dawsk

Erhu Kome Yellow

First Published in Great Britain in 2019 by
LOVE AFRICA PRESS
103 Reaver House, 12 East Street, Epsom KT17 1HX
www.loveafricapress.com

DEDICATION

This book is for the people dearest to me:

My sister, Odes, who loves this book more than I do;
The love of my life, Emmanuel, who supports my
dreams in every way;
Evelyn Kuluto who takes care of me like a daughter
and is always on my corner;
And my mother, Yellow, who left us too soon.

PROLOGUE

The western region, Nigeria
1875

The warm rays of the evening sun disappeared in the horizon.

The incantations began.

Maa bo pelu iji!

Mo pe agbara ti orun!

Mo pe ironse merin; tin se aye, omi, inan, ati afefe!

Fun emi ti o se dà wà ati eyi ton bo!

Gbo ebe wa!

Wa pelu wa ni ajo ti ale ji!

Lati ti ibi ro nitori ko ma ba le si lekun!

Ma se se wa ni ijamba mo!

Emi pe o wa!

From the east, the wind rose and whipped the trees, bending the branches and leaves. Dark clouds hovered over the Meje clan gathered in the forest clearing. The powers of the spirits they evoked with resonant voices surged in their midst.

The air reeked of a foul presence. Gusts of wind screamed, making the animals scamper in fright.

The hunters of Ori clan remained still and silent, hidden in the long grass, undeterred by the bloodcurdling sounds.

They had waited for this moment all their lives. This mission was the reason they existed, the reason they had been fiercely trained for years.

As devout worshippers of Yemaja, the earth goddess had imbued them with the strength to rid the earth of the abomination that tarnished her order.

The demon hunters with their bodies painted black and white, the symbol of impending war, had in their hands, daggers with long thick horns for handles.

These daggers had been forged from the rocks in the hidden cave beneath *Yemaja's* waterfall—the only weapons capable of slaying the beasts short of taking their heads off from their bodies, which proved to be an almost impossible task.

The hunters waited for the opportune moment to strike, their bodies primed for action, eager for the victory to come.

The Meje clan folk held hands firmly by the edge of the lake and chanted after their leader whose head was adorned with cowries and raffia palm.

Emi pe o wa!

Emi pe o wa!

A great whirlwind rose, startling everyone, including the hunters. It halted after a few heart-thumping moments.

A woman dressed in luminous white cloth materialised and settled gracefully on the surface of the water.

Her white eyes struck fear into the hearts of the Meje people, but their voices only became louder as they chanted without stop.

Thunder clapped in the distance.

The woman did not appear surprised by the events happening around her. She did not even try to escape when a cocoon-like substance began to envelop her body.

This worried the leader of the Meje clan, but they had to continue. There was no stopping now. They had risked their lives coming out of their sanctuary. They were already halfway to their goal of sealing the witch, and that was incentive enough.

As the chanting went on, the Meje people began changing to their true nature, a transformation which brought gasps from the hunters. Astonishingly, their bodies gradually transformed into beast-like forms.

At last, the cocoon swallowed up the woman and then it was slowly lowered into the water.

"It is done!" the leader of the clan, who had not transformed, spoke out in a loud trembling voice.

There were growls and high-pitched howling from the creatures.

A signal went up among the hunters. The time had come to fulfil the wish of their deity. The resonance of their war cries rent the air as the Hunters went out of their hiding places and laid waste to the people of the Meje clan who at that moment tried to salvage any strength they had left to fight back. The ritual had taken quite a toll on them

The stench of death hung heavy in the air as blood was spilt on both sides. One by one, the mark of the hunters, which linked them to the beasts, began to fade, which signified their task was at the verge of completion. The abominations would soon be wiped out from mother earth, and once again balance and order would be restored.

One of the creatures who found a path to escape ran off into the forest guided by the light of the silvery moon. It growled in pain as blood dripped from its side.

"Whatever is out there show yourself, be you spirit or man." A traveller who had found an abandoned hut and settled there for the night came out of it.

The noise among the bushes brought great fear into his heart. He picked a piece of burning firewood and moved forward.

The creature leapt out of the bushes and bounded for the man. It dug its fangs into his shoulders, and at the same time, they both fell to the ground.

The man shocked and injured remained on the ground. He was afraid the beast would come at him again and prayed to the gods of his fathers to save him. He waited for the final blow from the creature, but when none was forthcoming, he turned to his side. His eyes could not believe what he saw.

In place of the beast was a severely wounded woman.

CHAPTER 1

Orient City, Creek State, Nigeria
2025

For the third time this week, I stayed back to work a shift I hadn't bargained for.

Okay. Maybe I had.

Sure the doctors were bossy and the patients even bossier. Still, being a nurse at St. Cloud, one of the best if not the best hospital in the capital city, was very rewarding.

I loved my job. Maybe too much.

It was my most significant flaw and my greatest strength.

I stepped out of the elevator on the first floor and made my way to the lab. A voice stopped me when I turned right, heading down the chilly corridor.

"Nurse Simi." The attending paediatrician, Dr Izuchukwu, stood at the threshold of the door to a private room. The white patient chart in his hand looked like a cloud against his sky blue scrubs. "I need you to get the MRI results for Latifah Peters. Her mother wants to make sure she's not in any danger. I already told her it's just a bump and nothing more, but you know parents."

Yes, I did. I had to deal with them every day, answering their questions and listening to their complaints. Getting an MRI meant taking the elevator back to the fifth floor to wake up the attending radiologist, Dr Ezeogu.

"I'll get you the results soon," I told him.

"Thanks," he said and hurried off without looking back.

I took the elevator down to the floor, which held the MRI machine.

The patient was already in Radiology with her mother. The older woman held onto her daughter's arms as if the little girl would melt away any moment. I offered her a reassuring smile and waited for Dr Ezeogu to begin.

Begging the five-year-old girl to keep still so we could get a clear picture of her head was a task of its own. She kept squirming inside the MRI machine while her mother sang her a lullaby. Her mother offered her ice cream as a bribe if she remained still, but that did not work either. In the end, I had to administer a sedative.

Thirty minutes later, the radiologist handed me the results just in time for him to get back to sleep. I found the paediatrician and gave him the file.

My next stop was the nurse's station, where I had left my bag. I was ready to catch up on some needed sleep. I took the bag into the changing room and removed my scrubs, changing into a pair of jeans, a wrap top and sneakers. Casual chic and an off-and-on relationship with bohemian was my go-to style. I put my straightened hair into a ponytail and stared at the mirror right above the baby-changing table. I touched my jaw and groaned. Any skinnier and I would have to sign up with a modelling agency.

"I need food," I said to myself and made a mental note not to immediately lie on any flat surface when I got home.

Joshua waited for me at the nurses' station when I got out. I had completely forgotten about him. He was talking to Nadia, my colleague and best friend.

Joshua and I had been dating for three months, and he seemed to have understood precisely what my job entailed. He always did his best not to get angry when I had to cancel any plans we had. But he could only understand for so long.

With a pleading expression on my face, I walked up to him,

"I'm so sorry, Josh," I said and gave him a peck on the cheek, hoping it would ease his anger. "I know we were supposed to go out tonight."

"Three hours ago, Simi. Three hours ago. I had to leave the restaurant in shame and come here."

"I'm so sorry. I promise I'll make it up to you."

"When?" he asked with a scowl.

"How about tomorrow night?"

He shook his head and sighed. "I need to talk to you alone."

My heart sank. I glanced at Nadia who had one hand under her chin elbow on the desk, her ears perked up to catch every word we were about to say.

"Yes, we definitely need some privacy," I agreed, leading him by the arm to the main stairway.

"What do you want to tell me?" I asked when we were in the clear.

"Listen…"

"Oh no…" I said, my throat slowly closing up.

"I'm so sorry, Simi, but I think we should end this. I see no future for us."

When did a noose get around my neck? I could barely breathe.

"You're a gorgeous woman. I'm sure you'll find someone else. Or you could change your job."

I balled my sweaty hands and swallowed, hoping the boulder in my throat would go down smoothly. It didn't.

"I think you should stop putting work before men. Do you want to be an old spinster?"

I wanted to tell him to drop dead. Instead, with an icy smile, I said, "Thank you, Joshua."

"I hope ..." he began to say, but I was well on my way back to the nurse's station.

Nadia pretended to be buried in paperwork.

My body felt like jelly. My fists were still balled up, and my stomach knotted. I slowly looked up at Nadia.

"You can stop pretending," I told her.

"What happened? Tell me," she asked without hesitation.

I loosened my fists. "Nothing. Don't you have a job to do?"

She hissed and said "I don't care about that right now. Start talking, Oladeji."

"Like I said, nothing."

"Then why are you so sad? And look, Joshua is leaving."

I glanced back in time to see him push the glass door open and walk out.

"Did you guys have a quarrel? What did you say to him, he looked pissed?"

"We broke up, okay? He broke up with me. Are you satisfied, huh? Are you?" I meant to sound unfazed, but my voice betrayed me. My words came out like a child who just lost her favourite toy.

Her eyes suddenly went dim, and she gave me that 'what a pity' look I hated so much.

"I'm so sorry," She said, coming around to give me a hug.

"Why?" I sobbed against her chest. "I'm okay, right? I'm dateable, right?"

"Shhhh," Nadia's soothing voice tried to calm me down. "You're a hottie, you know that. Any man would be lucky to have you."

"But not Joshua," I said, spite rife in my tone.

"Not Joshua. Someone else."

"I don't want to be an old spinster."

"You won't be."

"I'm going home," I said, not wanting to draw any more attention to myself. I picked up my bag and slung it over my slouched shoulder.

"Yes, you should go home, dear. I'll call you."

I strode out into the cold night and walked down the street full of people going in and out of St. Cloud. I stopped at the T-junction, waiting for the tramcar.

Orient city was the first place in the country that had begun the use of tramcars. All thanks to Governor Ebeye, most of these streetcars operated in the shopping district. It was the best way for me to get from A to B.

I took the car at the T-junction and headed west for Darcy Avenue before taking a cab to Ugbe Boulevard where I lived in a sub-urban type cul-de-sac.

By the time I got home, my appetite and need to sleep had disappeared.

I spent hours sitting on the worn out couch, staring at pictures of Joshua and me on my phone. My heart pounded with every swipe. I noticed the delete button and started deleting in a rush. My hands were wound so tight around the phone, it switched off. I flung it, but it landed on the armchair across me unharmed. Even my phone gave up on me. I hadn't planned on crying, but I found myself bawling my eyes out until I fell asleep.

By the next morning, word had gone around St. Cloud that I had been dumped and was single and searching. I definitely was not.

I swear I could kill Nadia with my bare hands, but it was her default setting. She thought going around telling every male available I was single would make them respond like the predators they were, and that would boost my confidence.

Each time I walked past male nurses or doctors, they greeted me with stares. My face and ears burned with embarrassment. I wanted to hide, but I had to work, so I held my head up high and went about my business.

Halfway through my shift, I was making my way out of the coma ward when I was accosted by Dr Nicholas. He was one of three resident gynaecologists. His hands were in his pockets as he approached me. His long thin legs reminded me of a spider's.

"Simi."

My mouth fell open as I jerked my head, taken aback because he had never spoken to me. And now he was addressing me by my first name.

"Yes, Doctor Nicholas."

"You can drop the formalities, Simi. I heard about your recent breakup."

Of course. Nadia's gossip communication's system went wide, indeed.

"It's quite unfortunate."

"Yes, it is." The noose was back, and my palms itched.

"How are you holding up?"

"I am fine, thank you." The situation was becoming awkward with him standing in front of me and saying nothing.

"Do you need my help with something, Dr Nicholas?" Other than to talk about my damaged love life?

He hesitated before asking. "I was wondering if we could have dinner sometime. Tonight perhaps?"

Another awkward moment I had been hoping to avoid.

"Um…"

"It's just dinner," he persuaded. "What harm can be done?"

"I don't know, Dr Nicholas."

He took a step backwards and raised an eyebrow. "Call me, Nicholas."

"Right."

"I know you're not working late tonight."

That was true.

"So?"

"Okay." I forced a smile. "We can have dinner."

"I'll pick you up by eight."

"I'll be at the nurse's station."

He sauntered away and exchanged greetings with one of the orderlies.

It was fifteen minutes past eight when Nicholas reached the nurse's station. He was dressed in a casual long-sleeved shirt and black cotton trousers. He said hello and led the way to his car. I wore the knee-length kimono dress I got for myself on my last birthday tucked in the back of my locker and the sneakers I had planned on wearing home I regretted not taking the knitted sweater I had put out that morning. I hated the sight of Goosebumps all over my hands and legs.

"Cold night," I said, trying to start a conversation.

"Yes, indeed," was his input to my observation.

"Last year's Harmattan season wasn't as terrible as this year's. The night keeps getting colder and the day hotter."

"I imagine it wasn't. I was not in the country this time last year. I hate this weather; the extreme heat and the extreme cold." He frowned as he fumbled with his key.

We arrived at the restaurant at Bayside, a commercial district, after he drove for ten minutes. It was one of those old restaurants that had made a name for themselves when Creek state was formed. He ordered red wine to start, and we drank slowly.

"What happened to end your relationship so quickly?" he began.

"Work."

"Ha, I see. The great excuse."

"Yes."

"I'll get straight to the point, Simisola. I know it's too soon for you with your breakup and all, but we could have a good time."

I smiled at him if only to ease the increasing awkwardness of the situation.

"You're a lovely woman, Simi, any man—" He was cut short by the waiter.

"Are you ready to order?" He looked at me and then at Nicholas, who already picked up the menu from the table.

I stared down at the menu on my side of the table, not wanting to touch the darn thing. I let him order for both of us.

"We'll have the snail thing you have here. Is that good for you, Simi?"

I nodded.

The waiter left after Nicholas asked him to bring another bottle of red wine.

"As I was saying, you are..."

"You disgraceful adulterer!"

A woman in a blue blouse and pleated skirt shouted from the entrance of the restaurant. Everyone turned to stare at her. I wondered who she was and who she was referring to. And then I saw the fear in Nicholas' eyes and the way he tried to avert the gaze of the woman who was now strolling with determined steps towards us.

"Oh heavens, no..."" I muttered with my head down. "You're married?"

I had neither seen a ring on his finger nor heard anything about him being a husband.

He said nothing.

"Well, that's just fantastic."

The woman reached our table and gave him a slap that could be heard at the end of the room. "So the rumours were true. You seduce tramps like this one over here and have your way with them."

My hands trembled as she rained down insults on her adulterous husband and me. Was this a sign for me to give up on men?

"Eghe, I can explain," Dr Nicolas began.

"Explain what? Explain what, you bastard?" She gripped him by the collar of his shirt and spat in his face. That was not enough for her. She picked up the wine glass and emptied the contents on his head.

I could not hold back a slight chuckle. I laughed at the wimp of a man on bended knees, and at myself. How did I end up there? My eyes watered. I bit my lower lip to hold back the tears.

"We've only been married for two months, and you've already become a chronic adulterer. You have me. What else do you want?"

Dr Nicholas cleaned his face and said "I'm sorry. Let me explain."

"I want a divorce," was the last thing the crazed woman said before stomping away. Nicholas went after her, pleading woefully.

There was total silence in the restaurant.

I was too scared to look around. I could already feel the judgmental stares from the other customers burning uncountable holes in my body.

"Who's going to pay for the drinks?" The waiter was back.

"I'll... I'll pay. But just for the opened bottle." I gave him the money. I was ready to go when I heard someone say 'whore'. I called the waiter back. "On second thought I would like to have the second bottle."

I drank my wine at the bar, hoping it would drown out the voice that called me a whore. Whore? Really? Damn. I poured the drink down my throat to keep myself from retching. I finished the bottle and ordered another.

The person by my side who had been drinking slowly from a tall glass cleared his throat. I turned my attention to him. He was wearing a hooded sweater and jean trousers. He pulled down his baseball cap to conceal his face even though the dim light in the room was already helping him.

"Did you see what happened over there?"

I pointed in the direction of the restaurant. I was highly tipsy.

"I was disgraced, that's what happened. Embarrassed is the word."

He angled his body toward me, his face still hidden.

"A hard man is good to find. Wait, or is it the other way around?"

He appeared to be listening to me blab because he responded with a smile.

"I know I just met you, but I feel you should know these things. I am sad, stranger. I love my job, and it's constantly affecting my relationships. I'm never going to settle down. Maybe I should just concentrate on my job, you know? But my sister won't like to hear that. No, she won't. She's a crazy one, my sister, but she wants the best for me. No, I'll concentrate on my job."

He nodded slowly.

"I should. Yes, I should. I should have another drink."

I looked into my purse to find out I had no money on me and remembered I had left my phone charging in the nurses changing room. I laughed.

"Wow, no way to get home. No more money, no way to call for a ride. Aren't I just the unluckiest woman on earth?"

"I'll give you a ride home, Miss…" It was the first time I heard him speak, and I wanted to see the face behind such a soothing voice.

"Miss Simi, no," I waved my arms around sluggishly.

"Ice Queen." Hiccup. "Ice Queen is my name. My sister gave me the name, and it really is more befitting with the way I seem to put my job before my lovers."

I laughed and hiccupped loudly. "It's my superhero name. Shush, don't tell anyone."

"Can you write down your address?"

He gave me a pen and paper, and I managed to scribble down my address in handwriting that did not belong to me.

"Let's go," he said, getting out of his chair. I made to stand up, but my legs did a lousy job of supporting my drunken weight. The man was by my side, holding me up.

Big strong arms which could only be from so many sessions in a gym, half dragged me all the way to his car and put me in the passenger's seat. When he got in, he adjusted the cap on his head, and a stream of lustrous jet black hair partially spilt down his forehead. His hands reached for my body.

"What are you doing? What are you doing you, pervert?" I was ready to use my teeth on him if he tried to take advantage of the situation.

"I'm strapping you in, Ice Queen."

"Oh."

A sigh escaped from his full lips as he started his car.

"Where are you from?"

His eyes were focused on the road.

"What?"

"What country are you from, stranger?"

"Here, Nigeria."

The moving car and strawberry scent most likely from an air freshener made me sick.

"But..."

"My mother's German." His answer came out in a forced manner.

"I see."

He helped me out of the car when we arrived in front of my bungalow, the last house in the quiet cul-de-sac.

"Take care of yourself," he told me. I fumbled with my bag for a few minutes and finally found my keys.

"Thank you..." I turned around, but he was already gone.

***

It seemed like another lifetime when I found myself walking down this strange, lonely road, darkness closing behind me. The night seemed to be conjured out of the fog, clouding my senses and making me numb.

I did not recognise where I was or why I kept on moving forward. Soon I appeared in a forest. Falling leaves floated across to me and danced around the tall trees. I walked in and out of them baffled by how green and bright everything seemed. Behind a tree, about twenty feet from me was an outline of a person who hid as if afraid to get out.

"Who's there?" I asked, my voice shaky.

No answer.

I moved towards the shape, but it floated to the trees on my right. I turned sharply to find it gliding toward me.

It was a woman clad in white, holding a staff. She had a smile on her dark blue lips.

Trembling all over, I fell to my knees.

The sight of her terrifyingly white pupils should have sent me running, but my legs didn't move.

She came close, ever so gracefully and said, "Daughter of Ireti. The time is almost upon us."

"What ... what ... what ...?" I couldn't form words, and I blinked so fast I could barely see.

"When the time comes, you'll know," she answered. Her white eyes became black. "You'll certainly know."

She disappeared through the trees.

***

My body jerked as I woke to find my curtains on fire. I scrambled for the bottle of water on my bedside table and threw the contents on the flames. It went out with a searing sound.

As I stared at my charred curtains, my heart raced uncontrollably. I recalled the dream clearly. I knew not what to make of it other than a drunken delusion, but there was no explanation for the fire.

CHAPTER 2

The next morning, before my afternoon shift, I paid my sister and her family a visit. They lived in the government residential area, not so far from where I lived. I knocked at the door of the semi-detached building.

"Who's there?"

Jephery's voice came through the wooden panel. Jephery Eneje was my sister's husband and father to their twins; a man in his early forties who looked younger than his age even though he was already going grey.

"It's me."

He opened the door wide and beamed a smile. "Simi, my favourite of the Oladeji sisters."

"Don't let your wife hear you say such things now."

Chuckling, he ushered me in, locking the door behind me.

"Your aunt is here," he announced my presence to the twins.

"Aunt Simi!" the twins echoed as they leapt off the couch and rushed to my side for a hug, almost knocking me down. The girls were nearly twelve, but they looked sixteen.

"What has your mum been feeding you guys? Fertiliser? I need to get some of it."

They laughed and went back to their positions on the couch, both concentrating on their laptops. They had on their Spiderman pyjamas, making them look like mirror images of one another. It was challenging to know who was who sometimes.

No matter how hard I tried, I failed to differentiate them, so I came up with an ingenious system. "Lisa."

"Yes?" one of them replied.

"Good, here take my bracelet so I can identify you."

The other twin, Mona, laughed out loud.

"Who's out there making you guys laugh?" my sister called from the kitchen.

"It's your sister," Jephery said. He turned down the sound of the television and increased the volume of the surround system.

The voice of the sensational Rhythm and Blues singer Teju encompassed the room. After taking home two Grammy awards the previous year and another two this year, his popularity had skyrocketed.

Ava emerged from the kitchen, wiping her hands with a hanky.

Ava Eneje, my only sister and sibling and the centre of my world. She was a real African beauty with a smooth dark complexion and dark brown eyes that were hard to forget even after years or if you suddenly developed amnesia. Those eyes carried particular mystery about them you wanted to unravel if only to quench that burning curiosity.

After giving birth to the twins, she got rounder, making her even more beautiful. She was an epitome of sexiness, a quality I envied.

I somehow managed to remain stick thin despite my occasional binge eating. But I had my picture perfect eyebrows and creamy complexion going for me. It did not come cheap, though. What with all the skincare kits I bought every month or so.

"Mrs Eneje," I greeted, making myself more comfortable on the tan leather sofa.

"You don't look so good."

"I had a bizarre dream last night. Then there was the fire after."

"What fire?"

"My curtains spontaneously combusted."

"Dear Lord. Are you okay?"

"I'm fine. I was just as surprised too."

I'm sure it's the dryness. What's it called? Static on fabric, I think. The Harmattan is harsh this year. Everywhere is so dry."

"It's probably that."

"Have you been eating well?" she asked.

"Of course."

Her eyes narrowed.

"It's true. I ate a bowl of jollof rice before coming here." I lied.

"Hmmm," she hummed.

"If you want to blame anyone, then blame Joshua. I got dumped."

"What? Joshua broke up with you?"

Even the twins looked up.

"Yes. He could not handle my work hours. I forgot we had a date. It was the last straw, I guess."

"How did you manage to forget a date with Joshua?"

"I volunteered to work." My chest tightened.

Hearing myself speak, I began to think maybe it was my fault. I could have not volunteered to work and yet I did. From the wrinkle on my sister's forehead, it was clear she thought so too but did not want to say anything.

"Don't fret, dear," Jephery consoled me. "I did not like him, anyway."

It was the same thing over and over again.

"You'll find a better man," Ava said, putting her arms around me.

Something snapped inside me. I planned on keeping my depressing news to myself next time. Next time? My faith in the opposite sex and especially myself had diminished entirely if I was contemplating the next time I would get dumped.

"I'm sick and tired of men. They are all a bunch of cowards as far as I'm concerned. With you as an exception, Jephery."

"Thanks." He chuckled.

"Next time maybe I'll just hit it and quit it," I said with a sly smile.

"Simi! You cannot give up on men. I need to be your maid of honour. Don't you dare deny me the position, I beg of you. So you promise me you'll get out there and date some men. And certainly, no hitting and quitting."

I thought about it for a few seconds and was about to say no but seeing the expression on my sister's face, I had to say, "I promise."

"That's my girl," she said, and her gaze fell on her daughters. "Are you two done with your homework?"

"We are," they echoed.

"And?"

"We've sent it as an attachment to the teacher's email."

"The weirdo of a teacher," Mona added sniggering.

"Don't insult Mr Micah. He may behave strangely sometimes, but he deserves some respect, all teachers do," Ava told her daughters, who were chuckling amongst themselves. "And for the love of God, go and take your baths. We have to go to the supermarket."

They went upstairs, and my sister joined her husband on the couch. Lisa returned to retrieve her notebook.

"Lisa, can you help me with some water?" I asked.

"That's Mona,' Jephery said without looking at her daughter. My widened eyes fell on the girl who was now grinning. The joke was on me.

"Why do you girls always make a fool out of me?"

"And me," my sister added.

"Because it's fun," Mona snickered.

"How do you tell them apart, Jeph?"

"Fatherly instinct, I suppose."

"And what about motherly instinct?" I asked.

Mona interjected, "I think we were adopted."

"If you were adopted, why then do your eyes look like mine, you silly girl? Why do you have my straight legs and the exact same scar I have on my right shoulder?"

Mona hugged her mother.

"I love you, Mum," she said before bounding up the stairs.

"I love you too."

"What about your father? No love for him?" Jephery inquired.

"Love you, Dad." It was Lisa who replied from the top of the stairs, staring down, toothbrush in hand. "You too, Aunt Simi."

"Those kids. They never fail to make us laugh. And worry," Ava said with pride in her eyes.

I wanted children, but my recent run-ins with the species that made it possible for reproduction daunted my will. I left for the hospital after Ava and the kids went to the supermarket.

Later that day, Dr Ekwebelem, one of the new ER doctors, rushed to me as I filed in patients' records. I looked up at her from the computer as she tried to get all her words out at once. "We need you and whoever is available in the ER stat. Accident victims on the highway."

I hurried to the ER to meet a horrid sight.

There were so many people injured and fighting for their lives. Monitors once beeping went flat. Cries once heard went silent. The driver who was brought in with his head severely wounded, repeatedly shouted that he did not want to die. A few seconds later, a doctor called his time of death.

"Can you please attend to the patient in exam room five?" Dr Peters, another ER doctor asked. "He has been waiting for the past three hours. Finish up and get back out here."

He rushed past me to attend to a victim with a badly burned face.

"Sure thing," I replied.

As I passed the waiting room, I noticed two orderlies bringing a huge Christmas tree, with a bag of ornaments trailing behind them. It was the same routine every year. The Christmas tree was delivered a few days to Christmas, and then the carols serenaded the halls of the hospital; whether the patients or employees felt the jolly goodness of the holiday spirits or not.

I opened the door, and the patient who sat on the bed had his back to me. I needn't have looked at his face to recognise who the person was. His name on the chart had already given him up.

"Femi Bamidele," I gasped.

"Simi, Simi Oladeji? Is that you?" he asked with a wide smile.

"Wow," he added, hugging me with his left arm wound around me. Femi and I had attended the University of Ibadan. We were both studying Biochemistry for a year and a half until he left for some unknown reason.

"How long has it been? Six, seven years, I think."

"Seven," he stated.

"You've really grown. Now you have a moustache, and you've grown taller and bigger. Age suits you."

"No one thought I would, but I proved them wrong. But look at you, you grew up beautifully."

Femi had been a skinny boy who looked too young for his age. Most people had treated him like an adolescent, and he had hated it. Even with all his petite qualities, it did not stop me from admiring him or agreeing to be his girlfriend, making him my very first boyfriend. Now here he was looking incredibly buff. Life liked to play mind games on people. I took up his x-ray and examined it.

"I'll fix up your cast right away. You'll be using that arm in less than two weeks." His right hand hung limply from his shoulder, but he winced in pain as I examined it.

"Maybe we can catch up sometime and reminisce about old times. I just moved to Orient city though and know no 'cool' places. The only site I visit is my new home, in Ugbe Boulevard. Do you know it? "

"Do I know it?" I asked sarcastically. "I live there."

"What a pleasant coincidence. I guess I could drop by, say later today?"

I hesitated, but then I remembered it was Femi. Sweet old Femi. But one could not be too careful, after seven years, he could be a psychopathic killer on the loose.

"Yes, I guess you can." He took my phone number with a smile etched on his handsome face while I prepared to put a cast on his arm. Before leaving, he promised to call.

I went back to the ER, helping where I was needed. Within four hours, calm had nearly returned to the hospital, and I was hungry.

I scurried to the elevator in time to stop it from closing up.

The man in the elevator with the expensive-looking pitch black suit was headed to the same floor. His dazzling blue eyes seemed somewhat familiar. A warm cerulean blue. Standing a little over six feet and towering over my meagre height of five feet four inches, he paid me no attention. His left hand slid out of his pocket to reveal a ring with the initials too small to be seen.

"It's not yet visiting hours. You're here to see someone, I assume," I said to get some information out of him.

"I'm here to see Doctor Osayande." His voice was also vaguely familiar. His gaze was still fixed on the lights on the elevator buttons.

"The medical director? Why?"

"I need a favour from him."

"Oh."

He smiled at me then returned to staring at the buttons.

We were almost at our stop when I said "You look really familiar. I feel like I've met you before. But I would remember. Your eyes are peculiar."

This time his smile-slash-chuckle suggested he was in on some inside joke.

I could not make heads or tails why.

We both came out of the elevator and headed left towards the cafeteria. A lot of heads turned to stare at us when we entered the room. But I was not the one they were ogling at. It was my elevator buddy who now had one hand in his pocket and had unbuttoned his suit jacket. He was beckoned by Doctor Osayande who was already relaxed on one of the comfortable blue and apple-green coloured chairs.

I bought a sandwich and sat far away from them, watching them as they spoke to each other. Some of the female and even the male nurses kept on staring at the man who was talking to the medical director. It was clear as day to see why the female nurses drooled as they stared. The man looked like he just stepped out from a photo-shoot. Except it baffled me why the male nurses stared.

Nadia, who finally tore herself away from the liaison with the new male cardiac nurse, placed her tray of food on the table and sat next to me.

"How was the surgery?" I asked.

"She's going to be alright. Her husband has not left the chapel. He's still praying."

She looked up from her juice and tilted her head.

"Oh my god! Am I awake or asleep?"

"What?"

"What do you mean by what? Didn't you see him?" She pointed at the companion of the medical director.

"Yes, I did. He said he needs a favour from the boss."

Nadia laughed at me. "How do you know that?"

"He told me."

"Aiden Essien talked to you? Wait, what kind of favour would he be asking for? He already has everything."

Aiden Essien. The name sounded familiar. "Who's he?"

Nadia picked up the sandwich from her tray and took a huge bite from it. "I cannot believe what just came out of your mouth. Who is Aiden Essien?"

"You can't blame me for not knowing him. Must I know everybody?"

"He's a billionaire. Like a real one, not like those posers on Instagram. Come on, I'll tell you who he is." She brought out her new tablet from her purse and typed in Aiden Essien on the search engine and immediately, several pages sprung up. "He's the sole heir to the Jaeger fortune. He's currently the CEO of the Jaeger Group. I think Forbes named him youngest billionaire in Africa this year. I cannot believe you sometimes, Oladeji." She hissed and continued eating.

"Jaeger, isn't it German or something?"

"Yes, his father named his company after his German wife, Alexis Jaeger. Apparently, she was the only child, and her father had money like sand on a beach." I took the flat glittery tablet from her and scrolled downwards.

"The rich will always marry the rich and then get richer. Why do you think he named his company Jaeger? Marriage is a business deal to them," Nadia went on.

There was a picture of Aiden Essien that captured my attention. He was smiling, a sort of shy smirk with a couple of skyscrapers behind him. The smile was captivating.

Looking up from the tablet, I met his gaze. I glanced away as if I had been caught doing something terrible. When I turned back, Dr Osayande waved at me as if he wanted me to come over to them.

Nadia beamed, shuffling in her seat. I wanted to knock the excitement out of her if only to stop her from looking so childish.

"Dr Osayande," I greeted him and remained standing.

"Mr Essien, this is Simisola Oladeji. One of, if not the best nurse we have here in St. Cloud. Simi, I'm sure you already know who this is."

"Yes."

Aiden stood up and offered his hand. "Miss Simisola, I'm Aiden Essien. A pleasure to make your acquaintance."

There was that smile again. What was he smiling about?"

"Aiden has supported this hospital for a long time, although he prefers to remain anonymous. He is here with invitations to his annual Christmas Eve party, and he would like to invite you as well. You should count yourself lucky because you are the only staff member he's giving an invitation. You can meet me later in my office to get it."

Dr Osayande drank the dregs of his diet coke and stroked his rough stubble.

"Thank you, Mr Essien."

"You can drop the formality and call me Aiden."

"Ai...Aiden," I stuttered wondering why out of all the personnel in the hospital I was the only one singled out to be invited to a prestigious yet private party of such a man.

"The party will be held at my residence. The details are all in the invite. It will be a delight to have you."

"I'll be there, maybe. I may be occupied. But, thanks."

He looked amused by what I said and laughed lightly as I walked away.

"What did he tell you? Spill it, Oladeji." Nadia squeezed my arm so tight as if doing that would force the information out of me.

"He invited me to his party. On Christmas Eve."

Nadia's subsequent reaction to my words made me nervous. She looked like she was having a stroke.

"Are you okay?" It was my turn to squeeze her arm.

"Did you just say Aiden Essien invited you to his Christmas Eve party?" Her voice turned squeaky.

"Yes," I replied, finally taking the last bite of my sandwich.

Nadia let out a happy squeal that tilted a few heads in our direction.

"Shhhh." I hushed her, looking back at the people who knew not when to stop staring and mind their business.

"What was your reply?" she asked after calming down.

"I told him maybe I would attend his party."

"Maybe?" Nadia spoke in an alarmed tone.

I shrugged and said, "I may decide to come in here Christmas Eve." '

"But you are free that day and the next. The hospital will not collapse without you."

"Maybe it will."

"Damn," she huffed sadly. "You know you need this. You need to go out and meet new people."

"I'll think about it." I handed her the tablet from the table, and she placed it back in her purse.

"Look who just came in? The son of a bitch. Whenever I see him, I just want to wring his neck till every breath is sucked out of him. God will definitely punish him."

Nadia hissed like a snake as she threatened to murder Nicholas, in the hopes of reinstating my misplaced self-esteem from that regrettable night.

Nadia sometimes did not know when to quit, but she could murder anyone for me. All I had to do was say when. And it made me feel better.

In one swift moment, it all came to me when I saw Aiden smile, the shadow of a nurse passing by clouding his face. I had recalled bits and pieces but had doubted them. Now, it all made sense.

He got on his feet and steadily made his way out of the cafeteria.

I shot up so fast I made Nadia gasp and went after him.

"Mr Essien! Aiden!" I called after him.

He spun around gracefully and waited as I ambled towards him.

"You helped me that night."

"Yes, I did. You were pretty drunk."

"I never got to thank you. Thank you."

"You're welcome," he spoke, moving in the direction of the elevator.

"Where are your bodyguards? Are they downstairs?"

"What?"

"You've got a ton of money. I was just wondering why you're here alone."

He laughed. "No, I can take care of myself. Trust me."

How foolish.

"Why were you at the bar?" I found myself asking.

He placed a hand on his chest and answered, "Rich people have problems too."

A smile played on his bow-shaped lips.

"Why me?" I demanded to know.

"Why you?" He cocked his head.

"Yes, why invite me to your party? We've met once, and you can't call a drunken conversation a proper one."

"Because I find you interesting, Ice Queen."

"That's your answer? You find me interesting?"

"You don't like my answer?"

"Just being sceptical."

"To be honest, the invite was not meant for you, but after seeing you again, I strongly felt you should have it. It is much more preferable than inviting another old man."

"I guess I can accept that."

He tossed me a crooked smile.

"Goodbye, Simi," he said as he entered the elevator.

"Yeah, goodbye."

The invite was a brilliant silver card that had the faint smell of vanilla and strawberry. Accompanying the card was an expensive bottle of champagne. Nadia yelped and begged, almost going on all fours when she realised I was allowed to bring just one more person along.

"You have to take me with you, Oladeji. You have to."

Her eyes moistened with pretend tears as she pleaded.

"Alright, but I'm drinking the champagne."

It was exactly twenty minutes past seven pm when I left the hospital. It gave me ample time to go to the market and get the necessary items I needed to prepare my favourite food; yam and vegetable sauce. For a long time, noodles and a never-ending supply of toasted bread had been the only thing I ate. It was easy to prepare, and it filled my stomach. As I walked through the superstores that sold the needed ingredients for my food, my stomach growled disturbingly. I quickly bought what I needed and took a taxi home.

The CCTV screen on the wall and the lights came alive as I stepped into my living room space, a half-eaten chocolate bar in my mouth.

I took a quick shower and then got ready to cook. After an hour of sweating over the cooker, my doorbell rang shrilly as the song played from the surround system. It was my favourite song from Teju's new album.

I checked the screen to find Femi there, shifting from one leg to another. The doorbell rang again.

"I'm coming!" I yelled as I adjusted my blue slacks.

"You're right on time, Femi," I told him when I opened the door. There was a sweet smile on his face as he stepped in.

"On time for what?"

"Dinner."

"Oh yeah. I can smell your cooking. Smells delicious."

"Thanks."

I steered him towards the dining room, but he changed course and sat on the chair close to the kitchen counter, his arm rested on the dark green marble.

"How've you been?" he asked.

"Good. Where have you been all these years?" I asked as I set the table for two.

"I've been around. Been busy with countless things I never knew existed."

"Around is not a place. You just dropped off the face of the earth halfway into our second year. No number, no address or nothing."

"I had to leave on short notice. My parents are to blame really."

"Still…" I rolled my eyes.

"I tried contacting you, but you guys moved, and I could not trace you."

"Still…" I repeated

"I'm here now, aren't I?"

His question went unanswered. He flexed his arm as he stood up, and his dark blue cotton vest went up. A mark I once saw underneath his stomach years ago that was only a stretch of birthmark had become widened and more pronounced.

"What happened? It's larger now." I asked as he dragged the vest downwards to cover it up.

"Nothing."

His short mysterious answers only left me more curious.

"Nice painting."

Femi stared at the painting at the top of the wall in the dining room.

"This is one of my favourites, painted by the artist Ovo. Two others are in the living room. Have you heard of him?"

."I haven't."

"He's really famous. I'm surprised you don't know him."

He shrugged.

. "It's amazing how he captures people's emotions on canvas. Captivating is it not?"

"Yes, it is." Femi tried to sound interested but burst out laughing.

"I know nothing about art," he confessed.

"I won't hold it against you."

He helped me in bringing glasses and bottled water from the fridge and placed them on the table. We talked as we ate.

"I thought you were going to be a biochemist, invent an elixir of youth, discover some cure for something," Femi teased.

. "I find nursing rather fulfilling."

"Helping people has always been one of your strong points."

"And you?"

I emptied the water in my glass down my throat, surprised by my thirst.

"Believe it or not, I'm a private detective now. I actually got here to work hand in hand with the Orient City Police Department."

"No, kidding. "

"Yeah."

"What's the case?"

"I can't tell you."

"Why not?"

"Cause I may have to kill you."

"Ha, that's hilarious. You're a spy now? Tell me. I promise I won't tell anyone."

He studied my face carefully before speaking.

"Um, this is really hush-hush business. There's been a series of abductions. Three young women. All were taken at different times without any ransom being given. Two of them in broad daylight."

"Is there a connection?"

"None whatsoever."

"Wow. Who would have thought tiny Femi would become a detective?"

"Who indeed?"

He tried to hide his smile but failed to.

"This is absolutely delicious," he commented on the meal.

"Thank you."

"And how are your sister and her family?" Femi asked after a while.

"They're alright. The twins are all grown up now. I can't wait to let Ava know you're back."

"I really missed you guys, oh. To think we'd meet again like this. How random."

We finished eating and cleared the dishes.

"Dessert?" I asked.

"Yes, please."

I brought out a medium-sized chocolate cake from the fridge, one of the many experiments of my sister's that reached my grasp, and we ate in the living room. Femi spotted the card on the coffee table and asked, "What's this?"

"An invitation."

He read it. "Aiden Essien?"

"You know him?"

"As well as you can know a billionaire. You got invited to his party?"

"As you can see."

"You know him personally?"

"No, I don't."

"Are you going?"

"Yes, with my friend, Nadia."

He leaned backwards. "I don't trust these rich folks. They always have something up their sleeves."

"How are you sure Aiden has something up his sleeves? Are your detective senses tingling?"

"The rich are different," he answered.

Probably because they got all that money to spend and throw fancy parties.

"Of course."

His lips parted to form a smile.

"I really missed you Simi," he said, his voice conveying the truth with each word.

CHAPTER 3

By seven thirty pm on Christmas Eve, Nadia arrived at my place and blasted her car horn to hurry me up.

I put my hair in an up-do and squeezed my feet into a new pair of pumps which paired nicely with the sea blue flapper dress. I was pulling out my big guns.

Nadia did not hold back either. She went all out, from her makeup to her red dress and stilettos on her feet.

"I'm so happy you agreed to take me along, Oladeji," she said as she drove.

"It was nothing."

"Well, thanks."

When she sped up on the highway, I got carsick.

"Slow down, Nadia," I begged.

She chuckled silently. "Why don't you get a car, Oladeji? This public transportation lifestyle doesn't suit you."

"I hate driving, you know that."

"Is that one excuse?"

I ignored her question. "Besides, I could always use that money for something else. Buying a car is the least of my worries."

"What something else?"

"I'm saving up to travel. I even got my passport ready. I want to go somewhere beautiful, like Korea, or the Caribbean islands where I can just relax."

Nadia laughed out so loud, her body shook.

"Why are you laughing?"

"Wow. Joke of the century. You, Oladeji, you're going to travel?"

"Yes. I plan to next year."

"When you could not even leave your job for a night out with me?"

"This is different."

"Sure."

We arrived at Aiden Essien's Mansion thirty-five minutes later. It was located in a secluded area at the outskirts of the city on a windy hill surrounded by mahogany trees. His nearest neighbours were not to be seen because they lived about a mile or two from him. It gave the occupants the needed privacy and as Femi had put it, the perfect place to hide precious secrets up their luxurious sleeves. I handed the security guard at the gate my invitation before we were let through. He pushed a button in his hand. The gate slid open to let us in. Nadia drove in slowly, a twinkle in her eyes. Stepping out of the car, I took in the sight of my surroundings.

"This is one large property," I voiced out.

The mansion was designed in a modern aesthetic way. The massive pool looked like an artificial lake. It sat in front of the four-storied building that spanned a great length. A few steps from the low hedges was a fountain with water spewing out of a statue of a boy carrying a water pot. To the far left were two greenhouses and to the right a tennis court. Everywhere was lit in total brilliance.

Nadia and I took careful steps as we walked to the main arched entryway made of stunningly designed columns. I drew in a sharp breath of sweet smelling fragrances when the cold air from the foyer hit me. There was idle chatter from guests emanating from the den which definitely looked like a lounge. The place had glimmering pendant lights, coffee coloured couches, a bar running along the walls in a semi-circle and soft music coming from a grand piano.

"I feel like I died and I went to heaven," Nadia said.

"If that's how you feel, how do you think I feel?"

I moved over to the bar where I could have a clear view of the man on the grand piano. He had changed his rhythm and now played a jazzy tune.

"Are we still in Orient city?" I asked, not quite sure.

Nadia had already struck up a conversation with one of the men who stood next to the Christmas tree. It was apparent from the way he looked at her. He only wanted one thing from her. But she was oblivious to such, and even if she did notice, I was sure she did not care.

I wondered what her boyfriend would think about her flirting with another man, and so openly, without shame. I spotted the medical director talking with someone, his gorgeous wife by his side.

"What can I get you? Wine?" the male bartender asked me with probing eyes.

"No, thank you. I had a bad run-in with alcohol not too long ago. I'm still recovering."

"Some juice then?"

"That will be nice."

He poured some juice into a wine glass and slid it my way.

"Thank you."

He replied with a smile and dashed to his right.

"What can I get you? He asked the lady who walked up to the bar.

The waiters moved around, serving expensive looking drinks and finger foods to the guests. My eyes darted around, and I could spot one or two Nollywood movie stars having a laugh with other guests. Then I spotted a popular senator having a tete-a-tete with Aiden. It was the first time that night I saw Aiden.

Why did I imagine he would be waiting at the front door?

My eyes were fixed on him. I wanted them to wander, but like a magnet to metal, they were stuck to his frame. I was sure every woman in that room desired to be by his side, if only to bask in the self-confidence he exuded so effortlessly.

He turned around, and his gaze met mine. He abandoned his talk with the senator and strolled with poise in my direction.

I took in every bit of him from his hair to his shoes. His suit fitted his body so perfectly.

I gulped hard. "Hello," I managed to say. "You made it."

"Yes, I did."

My voice was unrecognisable to me. I was just glad I could still use my words and form them into sane sentences.

He leaned in and kissed my cheeks. "I was beginning to think you wouldn't show."

"I thought so, too, but here I am. You have a beautiful house."

"Thank you."

His smile unnerved me.

"Did you come with anyone?"

I wondered if he had asked me to know if I came with a significant other in male form.

"Yeah, my friend Nadia. She's the one standing over there looking likes she owns the place."

He turned around to look at Nadia, who was now busy talking to another man in a suit too small for his body.

"I hope you enjoy the party. You look lovely by the way," he told me. "Excuse me."

He was gone, and Nadia replaced him in a split second.

"I'm having the time of my life," she said, moving her head from side to side.

"I bet."

"Someone said there's going to be a magic show."

"Okay."

"What?" she asked, scrutinising me.

"Nothing. Nadia.

"Lighten up." She took rapid gulps of her drink.

"I'm gonna ask you a question, Nadia and you better answer truthfully."

"Go on."

"How many drinks have you had?"

She stared at the empty glass and said in a hushed tone, "This would make it my third. Or fourth."

"We just got here, Nadia. Why are you doing this to me?"

She laughed for a while and stopped when she looked at my face.

"You used to be better than me at this. I saw you one time doing that…"

"Don't you mention that," I said remembering the stunt I had pulled at a party with fire, a funnel, a two-litre jar of something called Aqua.

"You used to be the goddess of alcohol."

"Well, I'm retired now. I need you sober to drive me home."

"Are you sure?"

"What kind of question is that? Of course, I'm sure," I replied.

"I'm gonna go dance with that man."

"Don't get carried away."

Nadia waved her hand in dismissal and went back to her partner. When the charming waiter walked past her, she took another drink.

"Goddamit, Nadia," I swore under my breath.

"Hi, I'm Billy."

The blonde haired man with a neat moustache who walked up to me introduced himself. He offered his hand for a handshake, and I took it. He flipped it and kissed it.

"Nice to make your acquaintance, I'm Simisola Oladeji."

His brown eyes settled on my cleavage.

"You have the prettiest name, Simisola."

"Thank you, Billy. Are you a friend of Aiden's?" I inquired, forcing my hand from his grasp.

"No, just here for the sights."

It was evident he did not want to talk about Aiden. "You know I've been observing you from afar ever since you walked in."

"Is that so?"

"As a matter of fact, yes. I just have to say you are the most beautiful woman I've seen here tonight."

"Whoa, flattery. I thought that was extinct."

"No, I do not flatter you. I bet if your beauty were divvied up among ten girls, those girls would still be the prettiest girls."

"Now you're going too far."

"No." His voice sounded harsh.

"Okay. I believe you."

"Now we are acquainted, Miss Simisola, how about we skip this party and head for somewhere more private? Let's get to know each other better. Let's say my place, huh? A late dinner, some drinks and maybe breakfast?"

There it was. The annoying punch line to the whole joke.

"No," was my brusque answer. It startled him a little.

"It's just a friendly offer."

I almost told him to shove his offer up his rear.

"Yeah, I'm going to have to decline Billy. It was nice of you to come around and say those things and make your nice offer."

He gave me a twisted smile and picked up his drink. "You don't know what you're missing."

"I'll take my chances."

His grin died down quickly as he moved to sit alone on a leather sofa.

After the exuberant magic show by a man named Stevie Wonder, Nadia came running to me.

"Simi! Simi!" Nadia was almost out of breath when she got to me. "You will not believe who I just saw. It's IK. IK. Can you believe it?"

I refrained from telling her I'd already seen him.

"You have to come with me to talk to him. I don't know what to say."

I looked her over. She looked sober.

"Okay. I'll help you," I told her as an afterthought. I was afraid she might act too strange in front of him.

Ikponmwosa Best, popularly known as IK, was Nadia's favourite Nollywood actor. He was the classic example of the whole tall, dark and handsome package. But what Nadia admired most in the actor was his voice, a deep sonorous sound that made her melt each time he talked. So she said. The actor was just as he was on the screen only he was chatty. And not even the right type. For about an hour, he yapped about nonsensical matters and made rather dull jokes that made me want to rip my ears out. Nadia laughed at all his jokes, which I attributed to her being definitely under the influence: the influence of lust.

When the clock struck twelve, there were hollers from a few guests. Everyone wished each other a Merry Christmas. Even Billy came over to wish me a Merry Christmas.

"Are you sure you don't want to accept my proposal?"

"I'd rather die."

He walked away, glancing back at me a few times.

I could not find Nadia anywhere to wish her a merry Christmas. I searched for her in the confines of the party area, and after turning up with nothing, I broadened my horizon. One of the female waiters with short hair and massive breasts had seen her and pointed towards the entrance hall of the house. I continued walking and searching until I came to an area on the floor where it led down to a basement. A part of me wanted to go down, and the other warned against it. If anyone had spotted me staring down, moving from one foot to another, he or she would conclude I was up to nothing good. In the end, I chose to satisfy my curiosity. I ambled down the spiral staircase. It seemed to go on and on as if unending, but when I stepped on the last step, I was amazed by the view before me. Right in front of me was a hallway with a ceiling painted like the Sistine Chapel.

The first room to my right was the wine cellar. It was not a very large room, and it smelled a little like wood husk which made me want to sniff in some more of the air. My head snapped back when I thought I heard something move behind me. Of course, it was wrong to snoop around in someone's home, but by god was I going satiate my curiosity.

At the end of the corridor was a reddish brown door. It looked ominous. Something urged me to go back, to not open the door. Yet I found myself turning the handle and pushing. Part of me expected a horrific sight to come into view as I peered in. I breathed out and pushed the door wider.

The library was filled with so many books it took quite a while for my eyes to adjust to them. There was a step ladder leaning on the bookcases which stood from floor to ceiling running through the length and breadth of the room. It was dark save for the light from the lamp on the hexagonal table.

Libraries in people's houses were usually located at the living quarters, in the light. Why was this one here? Several books occupied the table and were bookmarked in several pages. I sat on the white leather chair and whistled. It was the most comfortable thing I had ever sat on. One of the books with a red hardback beckoned to me. On the front page was the title 'An In-Depth sight into the Realms of the African mythology by Professor Rufus Edem'.

On one page of the book, bookmarked was a drawing of a statue depicting the warrior god Sango. He had two long straight horns protruding from his head and held a sword with one hand and a decapitated head in the other side. Underneath this picture was a series of notes. I flipped the pages and found clippings of letters about the god Ikenga and the goddess Obba. There was another bookmark for the goddess Oyá. The last marker had less information about its topic. My eyes caught a white square door in between bookcases. I dropped the book back on the table and stood up, ready to fully satiate my curiosity.

What was behind the door?

I was almost within reach of it before I was arrested by a voice from the corridor.

"You shouldn't be here."

"I'm sorry."

The look on Aiden's face sent shivers down my spine.

"I was just admiring your library. It's really grand," I said, moving away from the door.

"You should not be here, Miss Simi."

"I'm sorry. I'll be on my way."

"Merry Christmas." His voice became less threatening.

He made room for me to pass through the doorway. I caught a whiff of his scent as my body brushed his slightly, and my involuntary reaction to this was a tingling sensation.

"Yeah, Merry Christmas."

"Can you..." His eyes conveyed sadness as he spoke. It baffled me.

"I'll find my way out, thank you. Sorry for invading your home. It was a lovely party."

"Thank you for coming."

I could feel his eyes watching me as I ambled my way up the staircase. It wasn't just about my snooping around his basement that ticked him off. It was something else.

When I got back upstairs, I found out most of the guests had already gone, and the few who were around were just the hired help who were cleaning up the place. Nadia's location still remained oblivious to me. I went in search of my purse and found it still sitting at the bar where I kept it. I fished out my phone and dialled Nadia's number. At first, it did not go through, but the second time, there was a ring. I patiently waited for her to pick up. The moment she did, I wasted no time in getting to the point.

"Where the hell are you, Nadia?"

"I'm busy."

"What did you say?"

"Oh, Oladeji, is that you?" There was a loud hiccup in the background.

"Yes, where are you?" I asked fuming.

"With Roland. He's such a nice guy."

Enraged, I almost shouted, "Who in God's name is Roland?"

"My new boyfriend. I met him at the party."

"What about your old boyfriend?"

"He's dead and gone to me."

I was asking all the wrong questions. "Where are you? Are you still at Aiden's house?"

"Not in the building." There was a shuffling noise, and I could hear Nadia asking her partner where they were. He gave her an answer.

"We're in..." she said.

I halted her.

"I know where you are!" I yelled into the mouthpiece. "How am I supposed to get home when you're halfway through town?"

"You can use my car. Oh, wait the key is with me. Sorry."

I ended the call before she could make out her unnecessary apology and tried to calm myself down. There was no use crying over spilt milk. I had to be solution oriented. There was no other choice than to get a cab on the road. I looked at the time. It was a few minutes past one.

I strolled down the hill, by the side of the road. A few cars sped by, but none stopped when I flagged them down. There were no cabs in sight, yet. I cursed Nadia silently for putting me through such a situation. My legs hurt from walking such long a distance on high heels. I had a right mind to pull them off and continue my journey with my bare feet, but all sorts of the dangerous objects could be lying on the ground, ready to snap at my leg.

A black Mercedes stopped after I flagged it down. A big mistake. Inside the large black vehicle were three men in almost matching attires and they appeared to be drunk. Yes, it wasn't Christmas until people succeeded in choking themselves with food, drowning themselves in alcohol and finally getting diabetes. The one in the back was sprawled halfway across the seat and did not turn when I spoke to the driver.

"Hey pretty, where are you headed?"

"Just down the road," I answered.

He and the scrawny man in the passenger seat laughed. The man in the driver's seat had to be the ugliest person I had ever seen, with two swollen lips and a scar running down his jagged face. The bling-bling around his neck did not help the issue at all.

"Come on, sweetie, are you headed our way?" he repeated. His breath smelled of alcohol.

"I'm afraid not. I'm sorry for the inconvenience," I said and resumed walking.

They drove up to me, and the driver stuck his misshapen head out.

"Let's drop you off."

"No, thank you."

"I insist," the man persisted.

"I'm almost at my destination."

"We insist," he said.

Ignoring him, I moved on, my head straight and eyes forward. When I heard the car engine stop and heard the car doors open and slam shut three times I froze. I forced myself to turn around, and I saw them, all three of them staggering as they progressed towards me.

Unconsciously, I doubled my pace and almost ran, but I had forgotten I was on six inches. The story of the abducted women came to mind. The men caught up with me in no time.

"You shouldn't run away from us, sweetie."

"Stay away from me!" I yelled, watching them cautiously. I took off my shoes and held on to them.

"Don't come any closer or else..." I warned, my voice shaky.

I aimed my shoes at them prepared to use it as a weapon in case they tried anything funny. Or not funny.

"We're not going to hurt you. We just want to give you a ride." The man who had been on the passenger seat laughed and his friend joined in.

"Like hell, you will. I'm not going to be merciful if you come any closer."

They circled me like vultures would a carcass before diving in for the feast. The one who had been at the rear seat reached for me, and without thinking, I used the heel of my shoe on him.

An offensive cry erupted from him, and I quickly bolted out of there before the other two men realised what had happened.

I ran like I had never run before. If those men caught up with me, I would be in serious trouble. I ran until I could no longer hear the pounding footsteps behind me. Although I suspected my rapidly beating heart made me partially deaf. All I could hear was the thumping sound hot in my ears.

The nearest house was almost in sight and hope soared in my heart. Fireworks erupted from the house, and the sky was filled with beautiful twinkling lights of red and gold and blue. I slowed down my pace, and the very next second, I was knocked down from behind. My forehead hit a rock. Thick, warm blood oozed out of the gash a little way above my right eyelet and trickled down my face. I kicked and clawed as one of the men forcefully turned me around.

"You bitch!"

"Let me go!" I screamed. "Let me go!"

But they were deaf to my words. The other man held me down. I fought back with all of my strength.

"Stay down, bitch," the man bawled. "You are going to pay for what you did to Matthias."

"Let me go!"

His gigantic hand fell across my face, and a sharp sting followed.

"This bitch has guts," the man behind the wheels said as he groped up my dress like an animal.

"Stop! Stop!"

The one called Matthias soon came around. He came straight at me and began kicking with brutal force.

I curled into a foetal position, a stabbing pain forming around my stomach. I was on the verge of losing my grip on reality. The blood flowed freely from my head, making me dizzy.

The driver pulled me up and tried to force his tongue down my throat.

I jerked back and bit off his ear. I was not going to relax and be raped by a bunch of animals.

He yelled out in pain as he held on to his bleeding ear. Shouting, he stared at me, madness in his eyes.

An unbearable pain ripped my right shoulder where he had successfully dug in his penknife. I stared at the small object stuck to me and wondered how such a little thing could inflict that much pain. My last ounce of willpower had been sucked out of me. There was no use fighting. I stopped fighting and resigned to my fate.

"Who's there?" Matthias asked.

The driver stopped tearing at my dress, and he too focused on the darkness.

"What is it?"

"I thought I heard something."

"It's nothing."

The blood had covered my eyes so much I could barely see. I was unable to move and quite sure some of my ribs were broken.

"Who's there?"

"There's nothing there, Mathias," was the last thing he said before the blood-curdling screams followed. It was difficult to see anything behind a curtain of blood and darkness. All I could hear was the shuffling of feet and someone saying "I'm not afraid of you."

There was another blood-curdling scream and then total silence. My eyes were forced out of fear to adjust to the darkness as I watched the colourful sprays of the fireworks exploding in the sky. Nothing could be done about my slipping away into oblivion. I saw a streak of something silver and heard growling like the sound a lion or tiger would make.

Then a familiar voice said, "You'll be alright, I promise."

The last things I saw were blue eyes before I fell unconscious.

CHAPTER 4

I was greeted by a sweet smell when I opened my eyes. Lavender or chamomile, I assumed. My surrounding was distinctively unfamiliar. The lights on the walls shone brightly, but I was sure it was daylight outside as rays of the sun tried to seep in through the thick lengthy curtains. The room was almost as big as my living room and bedroom combined. A walk-in closet with a glass door stood to my right.

The adjacent wall held a painting of blossoming amaryllis. I still did not know where I was. As if on cue, the events of the previous night came pouring in. I pulled the blanket off me hurriedly and searched my shoulder. There was no scar there, no indication I had ever been stabbed. I traced my finger across my brow, and there was no sign of a wound. The chalky silk night dress I was wearing was unrecognisable to me.

What happened? Why was I here?

My gaze went to the door and met a man standing there in the shadows.

"Oh my god! You scared me!"

"I am sorry," he replied and moved into the light. He was skinny but had a small rounded stomach protruding from his knitted sweater. His features were rough and sketchy on his creamy white complexion. His mouth was etched in a grimace as he looked at me. His scattered beard on his pimpled face reminded me of one of the orderlies in the hospital, only this man was quite older.

"Where am I?"

There was no answer from him. He pushed a button at the top of a switch and spoke into it. "Sir, your guest is awake."

"I'll be right there," came a reply from the hidden speakers. It sounded a lot like Aiden Essien's voice.

"He'll be with you shortly."

"What happ…"

He was already gone before I could finish my question. I waited patiently for his boss to show up. I had a lot of questions, and I needed answers. He came in sporting an ash-coloured sweater and white cotton trousers. His hair was a delightful mess.

"Simi," he said, almost affectionately.

"Mr Essien," I said, pulling up the blanket.

"Call me, Aiden."

"Sure, Aiden, what am I doing here?"

"You were unconscious, so we brought you here."

"Who are we?"

"That would be the angry-looking fellow you just met and me."

"Who's he?"

"His name is Henry Asyl. He's my assistant of sorts. He helps me out with things. Don't mind his serious demeanour."

"Fine. What day is it?"

"It's Christmas day. You've been asleep for a while."

"How's that possible? What happened? Last night I …"

Aiden came to my side and sat down. I edged away slightly.

My action brought a painful expression to his face.

His brows arched as he said, "you must be starving. You need to have something nice and warm in you. I already told Edna to get brunch ready by the pool on the terrace. Edna is my housekeeper in case you're wondering, and she's the same one who took care of your clothes."

"I'm not hungry," I replied with childish defiance. A rumble exploded from the direction of my stomach loud enough for him to hear.

"Obviously not. You have to eat."

I wanted answers to the numerous questions popping up in my head. Each more confusing than the next.

"Can you walk?" he inquired trying to find my legs hidden under the warm comfy blanket.

"Of course."

"Are you sure?"

"Yes, they are my legs, aren't they?"

When I tried to get up, I only succeeded in falling back on the bed. I had imagined I would be able to stand due to the amount of energy I had felt when I woke up. Damn. I stared at him shamefaced.

"I think you should eat in bed. You need to rest."

"I don't want to eat in here. I'd like to have some God-given air."

"Alright," Aiden spoke as if he expected nothing less from me.

He stood up and faced me, arms outstretched.

"What are you doing?"

"Taking you outside," he said and immediately scooped me into his arms like I weighed nothing.

I could not protest with those strong arms around me. He carried me out the door and up a staircase into a living room with wallpaper that changed regularly. The hall extended into the terrace which overlooked the mountainous region of Orient city. Green tropical rainforest filled the surrounding hills.

Aiden set me down gently on a chair beside the table where the food was set. Everything looked and smelled so good.

"Thank you."

"Coffee or tea?" he asked.

"Tea. I don't take coffee."

"Neither do I," he said, pouring the hot beverage from the teapot into a smaller cup.

He handed the cup to me and sat down in front of me before moving the sugar and milk in my direction.

"Do you have honey?"

He moved another jar toward me.

After adding a copious amount of honey, I took several sips from the cup and caught Aiden staring.

"Is there something on my face?"

"No."

"Aren't you eating?" I asked.

With his eyes still on mine, he picked a piece of star-shaped bread and took a bite. If that did not look like the single sexiest thing in the world, I did not know what did.

"Your friend came back to get her car. Nadia, is it not?" he asked, removing the lid to a dish to reveal a well-prepared omelette. He poured himself some tea.

"Yes, Nadia."

"She did not look so good."

"Why do you say that?"

"She kept muttering in low tones that she had a hangover."

"That's her. Did she come alone?"

"Yes."

My thoughts exactly.

"You're not eating," Aiden said.

"Sorry."

I quickly reached for more toast, wondering why I apologised.

"Eat a lot," he encouraged me by pushing the butter in my direction. "You need your strength back."

"What happened last night?"

He avoided my eyes, pouring his attention to the butter.

"Aiden?"

"We found you by the roadside and brought you here. I told you this. The doctor said you were dehydrated and tired."

"I was not. Something else happened out there." I pointed out into the horizon.

"Nothing else did I assure you. You walked a long way and must have been too tired."

He stopped avoiding my eyes and stared right back. He sipped his tea, leaning back on the chair. He hid his emotions so goddamn well I could not read him. I was sure something had happened.

"No!" I hit the table with my palm, spilling my tea in the process. "I was attacked by some godforsaken men."

I looked down on my shoulder. Nothing seemed out of the ordinary there.

"And you were there. Or I think you were," I said those last words slowly and quietly. "Someone or something else came along and helped me. Something." I realised how crazy I sounded.

"It was by chance we found you. You were unconscious, and your shoes were missing. No one else was there. We brought you here and called a doctor."

"I don't believe you. I mean, I couldn't have dreamed of being attacked and stabbed. The pain was real. I could swear I hit my head and was stabbed."

I was really beginning to sound like a lunatic. Maybe it was time to dial down the vehement protests.

"It could all be a dream, Simi."

"It's not. I'm not crazy."

"I know you're not."

"It was not a dream."

I wasn't giving up anytime soon. I tried to recall the events of the previous night. Nothing changed. Those blue eyes I saw put my investigation in a tight spot.

"Your sister has been calling all morning. I told her you'd call her when you woke up," Aiden said, obviously trying to change the subject.

"Why didn't you tell me?"

"I thought it wise not to disturb you."

"I have to call her."

"Are you satisfied? Do you want anything else?" Aiden inquired.

I stared back at the unfinished piece of toast in front of me.

"No, thank you. If you'd be kind as to take me back to my room I would be most grateful," I told him not even trying to check if I had regained use of my legs. He obliged my request, and in no time, I was back on the comfortable bed.

"Get some rest, Simi. I'll be back to see if you're better."

His voice regained that warmth I had noticed before.

"I still have to call my sister. I'll need my phone," I said realising I had forgotten about my reason for being back inside.

"Don't worry about it. I've had her number put into the house phonebook."

"What?"

He spoke into the surrounding, "call Ava."

He shut the door behind me. The sound of my sister's caller tune startled me.

"Oh." I gasped and smiled at my silly reaction.

"Hello," Ava's voice came from the hidden speakers.

"Mrs Eneje, Merry Christmas."

"Simi, is that you?"

"Yes."

"Merry Christmas dear, wait let me put you on speaker phone."

There was a click, and soon, the voice of the twins came up.

"Is it true? Are you really at Aiden Essien's house? Are you?"

"Won't you say hi to your aunt before you bombard her with questions?" Their mother reproached them. I pictured their excited faces and smiled.

"Merry Christmas, Aunt Simi!" The twins chorused.

"Merry Christmas."

"So is it true?" My sister asked.

There was a brief silence. I could feel them waiting eagerly for my response.

"Yes, who told you?"

"He called us to tell us you were with him. I did not believe him, so I had Jephery have a video chat with him. You must be thanking your luck the food you ate at the party gave you food poisoning."

"What do you mean?"

"Your food poisoning. And Aiden, oh he was so polite and humble, was so sorry about the whole incident. He didn't know the food was bad."

I guessed it was the story he had told them to keep them from worrying.

"Aunt Simi," one of the twins began, "when you get married to Aiden Essien, can Lisa and I come live with you? Pretty please."

"No one's marrying anyone," their mother said with a stern voice.

"It sure would be nice if we had a billionaire for an uncle and a cute billionaire uncle at that."

"Mona!" Ava's voice came out harsh.

"Mrs Eneje, stop the yelling. Kids will be kids. Mona, I barely know this man. I'm his guest because I'm too sick to come home."

Lisa asked, "When will you be back?"

"Tomorrow. And don't worry. I'll bring your presents along."

"Thanks, Aunt Simi," came another chorus.

"Where's your hubby?" I asked, remembering the gang was missing a male voice.

"He's out with one of his friends, you know Alex, right?"

"Yes, the one with six fingers." I could my sister frowning when I chuckled.

"Is that all you remember of him? He's handsome and wealthy. And you know he's had his eyes on you for quite some time."

"But not as handsome and not as wealthy as Aiden Essien!"

"Mona leave here!" my sister screamed.

I laughed out loud and almost fell out of the bed.

"Simi, you have to give love a chance."

"I've heard you."

"I know you when you say that it usually means the opposite."

"I've heard you," I repeated.

"You have to see grandpa tomorrow. He's really missed you."

"I will. Send my greetings to your hubby."

"For sure."

The click sound from the other end terminated the call. I looked down on the blanket and made a mental note to pay my grandfather a visit. Then I tried to piece together the events of the last 48 hours and came up short. Why would Aiden lie to me? Where did my injuries go?

Several hours later, I awoke from a long nap and felt revitalised. I tried using my legs and found out they were working, but I still felt weak. Walking over to the curtains, I slid them open to find the sun gradually sinking into the sky. I moved away from the window and walked out of the room, closing the door gently behind me.

The wide corridor seemed unending. I took to my left and followed it until I came to a room whose door was half open. The room had a dome-shaped ceiling from which hung bright yellow teardrop pendant lights. It also had an artificial fireplace where the fire danced about. Above the fireplace was a large painting facing the magnificent king sized bed with cream pillows and a brown duvet. I was drawn to it and nearly entered the room but had to step back when Aiden walked to the bed and laid out a white shirt. The only item of clothing on him was a velvet slack which slid down his inguinal crease.

Looking that fine was wrong. Just so wrong. Aiden glanced at the door, but I was faster. I made for the stairs.

No one saw me thank heavens, but the front door opened to reveal a man, probably in his early twenties. He was lanky and of average height. Nothing about his physical features made sense. His eyes were too narrow for his broad forehead, and his head was oval with ears like elves.

"Hello. Good evening." He grinned as if just being in my presence made his life better.

He held out his hand, which I took. His flat hand surprisingly had a firm grip.

"Mrs Essien?"

"No."

"Fiancée? Girlfriend?"

"No relation, just a guest."

"Oh." He seemed disappointed. "Is Mr Aiden around? I was asked by him to bring these over."

He showed me a black file.

"Who are you?"

"I'm Lawal, Seyi Lawal. One of Mr Aiden's aides. Well, not aides. More of a glorified intern. He's home, right?"

I observed him closely. He did look like an assistant. He was bent on putting up an impressive appearance. His hair was neat and beard well-trimmed. His red tie was straight and narrow swinging across his well-ironed white shirt and black trousers. His meticulously shined shoes ended the whole get-up.

"I'm here to give him reports on some of the happenings in his factory in Orient City and some matters concerning a few workers. I rarely get to see him, though. The last time I saw him was at his steel factory in Port-Harcourt. This is the first time I've ever been to his house here in Orient City. It's a beautiful place, is it not?"

"It is," I replied, slowly moving away from his radius. His voice pulled me back.

"Did you know this house was built in less than six months? Hard to believe is it not, but it's true. The..."

"Lawal," Aiden called from behind me. "Don't drive my guest away with your lectures."

"Sorry sir, Mr Essien, sir."

Aiden glided down from the stairs gracefully and came to stand by my side. He was wearing a sports shirt now. Lawal stood there, smiling sheepishly at his boss.

"Lawal, the reports."

"Oh sorry sir, here they are."

He handed the papers over to him.

"I'll call you when I'm done with them."

"Yes, sir."

"Goodnight Lawal."

"Goodnight sir and I just wanted to say I read your interview with BUSINESS DAILY. Your words were such an inspiration, sir."

"Thank you, Lawal."

"Yes, sir," he said finally and left.

"I think he's in love with you," I stated.

"Lawal's a bit strange, but he's eager to learn, and he gets his job done to the letter. I see you're strong enough to walk and spy on people." He looked at my feet.

Maybe I wasn't so fast after all.

"Yes, quite. And I wasn't spying."

"Dinner will be served at seven-thirty."

He headed up the stairs and disappeared into his room.

I met a robust woman in a denim skirt and a blouse laying out a dress on the bed when I stepped into my allocated room. Her face was round and her eyebrows thick, but it only succeeded in bringing out her peacock green eyes. Her brown/grey hair was in a bun which suited her smiling face perfectly.

"My name is Mrs Edna Patty, but everyone calls me Mrs P."

"It's nice to meet you. I'm Simisola Oladeji."

"Ooh what a pretty name. I was astonished when....." She giggled. "Mr Essien doesn't bring any girls home. Never has. But you sure are a catch."

"Thank... you. How long have you been working here?" I asked, hoping she would be open to answering more questions. I could use whatever information I could get. "For as long as I can remember." She tipped her head upward when she answered. She smiled as she said this. "What do you do dear?"

"I'm a nurse."

She let out a light squeal. "A nurse, how wonderful!" Her tone conveyed it was.

"And how long has Mr Henry been here?"

"For a very long time. Mister Essien asked me to bring this to you."

She motioned at the dress on the bed. "I bet it'll look marvellous on you."

"I'll bet…"

"I'll leave you to clean up now. I'll be back to show you to the dining room. With so many rooms in this house, one may get lost," she said and left.

That went well. I ruled out Mrs P from my list of people to interrogate. Perhaps I could find another maid to interview. Or Henry himself.

Mrs P came by just as she had said and led the way to the dining room.

"My dear, you look absolutely stunning."

Then she used the word radiant and then warm on the eyes after subsequent pauses. The dining room was at the end of the hallway hidden behind the bottom of the grand staircase. The floral tiled floor blended with the long curtains which were thrown open. The crystal chandelier hung low over the oval dining table where a banquet had been laid out. Aiden stood beside the table, arranging the centrepiece vase which held flowers of shades of blue, white and pink.

He looked up and said, "You look stunning," a warm, inviting expression on his face. I looked down at the dress.

"Just as I said," Mrs P chimed in.

Aiden thanked her, and we watched her leave. He came over and pulled the chair out, and I sat wondering if such manner of chivalry existed anywhere outside that room.

"Do you want to fatten me up for a sacrifice, huh?"

Aiden opened a round-bottomed bottle of wine and poured some into my glass.

"How do you feel? Are you better now?"

"Yes, I can leave today."

"I'd rather you do not. You can stay one more night. Tomorrow morning, I'll have Wallace take you home."

"If you insist."

I watched him through the corner of my eyes as we ate. He cut the grilled fish and potatoes in front of him and chewed slowly.

"You've been staring Simi."

His voice startled me.

"I wasn't. Okay, maybe a little."

"Why?

"Nothing. Okay, maybe something."

He laughed.

"A little birdie told me you don't have much lady friends over, and it baffles me how someone like you could avoid not being suffocated under a pile of women every day."

With an eyebrow raised, he asked, "like me?"

"You know what I mean; young, rich and handsome."

Strikingly beautiful should have been the words to use.

"I haven't really thought about it. Well, you're a woman, and you're here, so that counts for something."

"Hardly."

"It does. A whole lot."

"How?"

"It's complicated."

He was evasive again.

"I've had flings here and there, but nothing sticks. I know you must have broken a few hearts and then some more."

"More like the opposite," I replied with a mirthless laugh.

He cocked his head and arched a brow.

"Story for another day," I said.

"You talked to your sister, I suppose."

"Yes," I answered, remembering the awkward conversation. "She's less worried now although I doubt it."

"Why?"

"Big sister syndrome."

"Ah," he muttered. "You told her I had food poisoning. Why not just tell her I was found on the side of the road, passed out?"

"I figured she would have a panic attack. Big sister syndrome, you see," he replied with a smirk. "It must be nice to have a sister. I always wanted a brother."

Two Aidens? I imagined women falling over as they walked by.

"We would have conquered the world together," he joked.

"I bet."

After dinner, we slowly emptied the bottle of wine.

Aiden cleared his throat and said, "last time you were in my house, you were snooping around."

I hid my face away.

"I could not help myself."

"How would you like to see my favourite section of the house? It may yet satisfy your curiosity about me."

I wanted to say I was not curious about him. That would have been a lie.

"I would love to," I replied, suspicious of his reason for his request.

"Come on," he said, putting down the wineglass.

As we walked towards a closed door at the back passageway, he lowered his voice. "This house was designed after my Grandfather's in Northern Ireland. Only the land area is not as big. Every single detail was not left out except this."

We got to the front of the wooden door, and he pushed a button by the side of it.

"I thought an elevator would give a better entrance to the place we're about to enter. A staircase doesn't do much justice to it."

I asked as we ascended, "how many rooms are there in this house?"

"20."

"And how many have you been in or used?"

"Probably less than the amount you're thinking of right now."

"It must be pretty lonely."

"Sometimes. But I've got Henry and Miss P. They're like family."

The elevator came to a halt, and the doors slid open. The gallery spread open before my eyes. The numerous canvasses with portraits were lined up on the white wall that seemed to lengthen and merge into an endless path. Dumbstruck, I ogled at the painting at my right.

"This is wonderful," I spoke up at last.

"The gallery extends up to the third floor. My grandfather was a collector of famous portrait paintings. I, on the other hand, collect what I fancy. And some that could become assets." Aiden walked carefully beside me but not close enough to disorient me. I noticed a painting and stopped.

"I know that painting. It's Ovo's, isn't it?"

"You know your art."

Aiden sounded impressed.

"I only know Ovo's art truth to be told."

"It's a start," he said, smiling down at me.

I trailed my finger on the painting staring at the doleful eyes of the young boy who had a fading sneer on his face. His face almost covered the entire canvas. Behind him was a mud hut with a battered thatched roof.

"It is gorgeous," I whispered.

I turned to glance at Aiden to find him staring at me, lips parted slightly, a smile dangling at the edge of his mouth.

"What is it?"

"Nothing," he replied, then paused before asking "how do you usually spend your Christmas? Not browsing through private galleries, I presume."

"No, I usually spend it with my sister and her family. We'd go out and do something fun, and when we get back, my nieces and I would have a movie marathon until we fall asleep."

"And?"

"And sometimes," my gaze returned to the painting, "my grandpa would visit. He's a delight."

I remembered I had to go see him.

"And your parents?"

"Dead."

"I am so sorry."

"Don't be sorry."

"I know how you feel. But you have your sister and your grandpa, which is something."

"I am lucky."

He was silent for a while. He placed both hands in the pocket of his slacks and leaned against the wall while I admired the sketch of a ballerina.

"When I was young I spent my Christmas at my father's house in Calabar and sometimes at my grandfather's in Germany but right now I celebrate it with my face buried deep in work."

"You have no family you could spend it with?"

"My mother, but she's another story for another day."

"Your father, how did he die?" I asked.

"You're the first person who's ever asked that of me. As for others, their phones or computers would be their first choice."

"I'm not others. I am glad to say I have resisted the urge to go about researching you."

"Why?"

"I think I much prefer this. No filters."

"I prefer this too. My father, he died of a heart attack. Didn't think that was how the old man would go out." He chuckled loudly.

"I'm sorry."

His warm hand fell on my shoulder for a brief moment. He squeezed slightly in a bid to let me know he was alright. He gestured for us to move forward.

We arrived in a secluded section of the gallery. There was a single portrait on the wall. Although the woman had only the right side of her face shown, anyone could tell she was incredibly beautiful. Hair face was straight and slim, ending in a strong chin. She looked like she was giving someone unseen a scolding but in a loving way. Her long blond hair fell flawlessly down her back and on her red dress. There was something familiar about her. Then I saw it.

"Is that...?"

"My grandmother."

"She's a knockout."

He moved closer to the portrait and smiled.

"She told me she didn't want to get her portrait done but was convinced by my grandfather who promised to do a naked portrait of himself and then she agreed."

"Did he? I mean not that I want to see it."

Aiden laughed in a way that soothed my uneasiness completely.

"Don't be scared. He didn't do it. He tricked her, but when she saw this," Aiden pointed at the painting, "she didn't mind being tricked."

I scrutinised the portrait again, seeing much of Aiden in her with every look.

"You're not going to tell me what really happened out there are you?"

The words came out like water from a damaged pipe. I had not planned to ask him there and then but the cat was out of the bag.

"What?" he asked, his brows knitted in a growing frown.

"Your story about how you found me out by the roadside sounds pretty farfetched."

"It is not."

"What are you covering up?"

Aiden backed away, giving me the same threatening scowl he had given me in his library.

"Why are you irrational?"

"I am not. You're the one who is."

He looked like he wanted to shake me until I gave up asking any more questions.

He groaned and said, "I don't know why I'm so drawn to you."

"I did not ask you to be," I snapped, although his words made my heart flutter. "I think I should get back to bed. I'm tired."

"Perhaps, you should."

His wide sullen eyes almost made me sorry for my attitude. Almost.

CHAPTER 5

I was back in the comfort of my own bedroom shortly after the sun came up on Boxing Day. Aiden had seen to it that I got back home safe, but I had not seen him before leaving. Henry only gave a grunt of a reply when I asked about his boss' whereabouts. After which he handed me my phone and my purse. I took that to mean my presence was no longer appreciated.

I chewed on my lower lip, irritated by the raspy knocks on the door. I opened it to find Femi looking worried and worn.

"Where have you been Simi? What happened to you?"

"Nothing."

"Don't tell me it's nothing, I called your sister when I could not find you yesterday, and she told me what happened."

I did not bother to ask how he got her number. It was just like Ava to go about telling Femi what should clearly be a private affair. She had always taken a shine towards Femi ever since I introduced them to each other years ago. She had had silly notions in her head that we'd end up together, matrimonially. I could bet those notions came right back when she heard his voice again.

"Of course you did. I'm fine. Thanks for worrying."

"I told you not to go to that party, but you wouldn't listen."

"Next time I'll heed your advice. I just have to rest," I told him smiling if only to make him go away. He got the hint.

"I'll leave you now, but be careful."

"Alright. Thanks for stopping by."

I made sure he was far off before heading back into the house to prepare for the journey I was about to embark. The cab I called to take me to my destination arrived in under an hour.

"We'll make a stop at GRA first."

"It will cost extra, oh."

"I'll pay."

"Okay, ma," he said before starting the car.

I met my sister and her family trooping outside their home and heading for their SUV.

"Aunt Simi!" The twins shouted excitedly.

"Hey, munchkins, where are you guys off to?"

"The mall!' they chorused.

I handed their presents over to them and watched them scream.

"Are you not coming?" their mother asked.

"No, I'm on my way to see grandpa."

"That's good. Say hi to him for me, okay?"

"I will."

A grin came out from the blue and clouded her face.

"What?"

She nudged me and winked and raised her brows several times. "You think I don't know?"

"Don't know what?"

"Femi. No wonder you rejected my matchmaking gesture for you and six-fingered Alex."

"No."

"You can't even deny properly."

"I'm leaving," I said.

Jephery came out of the house squinting as the sun hit his face.

"Hello Jephery, bye Jephery," I said quickly and took the long walk back to the cab sitting by the roadside.

"Bye, Simi," Jephery called after me. I waved without looking back.

***

The house Ava and I had lived in with my grandfather when growing up was a bungalow with an asbestos roof with just three rooms; a small but comfortable place in a serene environment. I braced myself for what I was going to see. The living room had not changed. Most of the furniture was made by my grandfather, who had a way with wood and cane.

On the mantelpiece were carvings of little men in canoes and a couple dancing. It still held pictures of Ava and me as children and of my parents.

My parents.

I stood staring at the picture of my father and mother on the wall. My hand wanted to reach out to touch them. I knew better than to do that. It would only bring back pain. It felt like yesterday when the news had come of their demise. The car had skidded off the road and hit a tree. They had both died instantly.

"Simisola, my beautiful child."

My grandfather walked into the room with his arms held out.

"Grandpa," I greeted and went halfway down on my knees, but he quickly raised me up. His trembling hands were wrinkled and full of veins. My father had been his spitting image; they had the same brown hair from which my grandfather had refused to let go at his age, thin eyelashes, and incredibly white teeth.

"So very beautiful. I remember when everyone kept on calling you Abiku as a child, and you thought that was your name. Do you still get sick as often?"

"No grandpa."

"Good," he grinned. "Sit."

He offered me a sofa, and I gently eased into it.

"Merry Christmas grandpa. I would have got you a present, but my plans took an unexpected turn. I'm..."

"You don't need to apologise. Your presence is already a gift. How is work?"

"Work is good."

"And you?"

"Never been better."

My eyes found their way to the picture on the wall, and I winced.

"What about marriage? You're not thinking of settling down yet?"

It was one of those things I liked about my grandfather. He never wasted time to get down to business and say what he was thinking.

"No grandpa. It's not really on my mind."

"But it should be," the old man protested. "It should be. Your sister already has two kids."

"I know."

"Don't you want children of your own Simi?"

"I do, but I've not found the man worthy enough to be called husband."

The old man sniggered. "When I married your grandmother, I only knew her name, nothing else about her. Neither her hobbies nor what she liked. But after years together, love came into the equation. I know you youngsters want to fall in love, but other factors still apply."

"I will never agree to an arranged marriage."

"I know you too well to suggest that." He settled more comfortably on the sofa. "You're just like your grandmother."

"I've heard that before." From my mother.

"When your parents found each other, we all knew it was a match made in heaven. They were an exemplary couple."

The old man sighed and came to sit beside me.

"You need a husband," he said, and that got me laughing. "I'm serious."

"I'll look for one. Even if I have to drag him to the altar," I joked.

"Are you hungry, Simi? I have fish stew and rice if you are."

"I'm not hungry grandpa, thank you."

I decided to ask. "Grandpa…"

"Yes?" His voice was laced with emotion. I could tell he had been thinking deeply.

"What do you know about the god Sango?"

"Why…"

"I just want to know," I told him trying to sound vague.

"Well, I know he's the god of thunder and lightning in the Yoruba religion. He's the most popular Orisha or a god among the others." He spoke slowly, counting each word. "Sango was also the third king of the Oyo kingdom, and he married three wives. There is a popular tale involving the first and second wife. I'm sure you've heard of this story."

"I read that story from a textbook in secondary school."

"Yes. The second wife Oshun out of jealousy tricked Oba the first into using her ear to cook for Sango. She was driven away by him because of this."

"And what about Oyá?" I asked.

My phone rang, it was Nadia. I ignored it.

"That would be Sango's third wife. She is popularly known as the goddess of magic, the Orisha of change. She is a warrior goddess dand very powerful. And it is said that she brings about destruction through her ability to cause storms, tornadoes and hurricanes alike. My grandmother was a devout worshipper of Oyá."

"I did not know that."

"I remember when she would dress in white and do her rituals. Her usual sacrifices were eggplants, to her mother of nine as she liked to call her. The goddess was called 'Mother of Nine', Oyá–Iyansan because the Niger River is known to have nine tributaries. My grandmother also had nine marks on her face."

"That's fascinating."

"It is good you are asking all these questions. It is good to know your roots." He paused. "Do you have any other questions?"

"Yes... what do you know about people who turn to beasts? Shape-shifters. Like werewolves."

"I don't know about werewolves, but I do know about an old Yoruba tale of 'Were-Hyenas'. These beasts were called Kpelepke. They usually preyed on cattle and sheep, even humans. These men and women would turn into their beast forms and howl in the night to compel people to meet them in the bush so they can eat them."

"Is that true?"

"No, all these creatures are mythical. They were tales my grandmother told us, children, to keep us inside the house at night."

Myths are born from the truth I nearly said out loud. I did not want to tell him about what happened to me and what I suspected. Shape-shifters in Orient City? It sounded so ridiculous.

"Why all these questions? Are you taking a class in African studies?"

"No grandpa. I was just curious."

I rechecked my phone to find a text from Nadia telling me to come to the hospital if I could. She said she needed emotional support, and the hospital needed extra hands. Nadia knew me well. She knew I would come once she mentioned the hospital.

"Grandpa I have to go."

"You're not staying?"

"No, but I will make sure to be back before New Year."

"I will be at your sister's house for the new year."

"Even better."

He stood up with me but only at a slower pace and I could see how much age had affected him.

"This back is not what it used to be," he commented laughing. On impulse, I hugged him, and I was a little girl again holding on to him for protection from Ava. I smiled when that wave of nostalgia washed over me.

"Oh my child," he said in between chuckles. "God bless you."

"Thank you, Grandpa. I'll call you when I get home."

On my way back to Orient city, in the cab and staring out into the terrain of the countryside I thought about all my grandfather had spoken of, and one question kept bugging me; Was Aiden a Shape-shifter?

CHAPTER 6

The New Year celebrations came and passed quickly. I had no resolutions because I didn't think anyone needed it. If you didn't start your weight loss journey in December, then you won't in January. It was time to settle back into my job. It took my mind off other things; a welcoming situation I relished. Nevertheless, I dreaded what was to come the following month, but just like death, it was inevitable.

Two days before Valentine's Day, nearly everyone in the hospital already had its fever. Flowers exchanged hands like it was money, and the chocolates were abundant.

"I don't see any reason why you should pick out one special day to commemorate your love for someone," I said to Nadia and Nurse Onyeka who were with me in the Nurses' station that evening. "Your love should be shown every day."

"Valentine's Day is my favourite day," Nadia announced.

"Mine too," Nurse Onyeka added. He was staring at a girl who seemed to be lost in the waiting room. "I'll be back."

He walked up to the girl and whispered something into her ears, and she laughed.

"Valentine's Day makes me sick," I spat.

"Of course it would. I remember the exact Valentine's Day when this jaded thinking started."

Nadia had been there when it happened. A break up on such a special day for lovers tends to remain in one's memory for a long time.

"Valentine's Day should be banned." I did not give up.

"That's just your loneliness talking,"

Nadia laughed, handing me a patient's file. A young boy no more than nineteen parading a wide-brimmed hat walked in carrying a bouquet of flowers in his arms.

"You see that?" I pointed at the boy. "Obligations upon obligations."

Nadia let me ramble on.

He walked up to us and asked, "Is Nurse Simi on duty today?"

"Who's asking?"

"Mr Femi Bamidele asked me to give her these."

Nadia was trying her best to hold back her laughter.

"I'm Simi. Thank you."

I took the flowers from him.

"They're beautiful," Nadia said, laughing out loud now.

"Don't tease me. I'll send these back."

"You will do no such thing Oladeji. Give them to me."

"Don't bother yourself. I'm keeping them."

I searched around the flowers and found a card. It read 'Happy Valentine's Day in advance, Femi.'

"Is it the same Femi you told me about? Tall, dark and handsome?"

"Yes"

"Wow, he must really like you. He must really like you in a Valentine way."

"You're mad."

As I pondered on the reason that prompted such behaviour from Femi, another surprise came walking through the front door of St. Cloud.

"Oladeji, it's Aiden Essien," Nadia let me know.

He looked debonair in his navy blue suit. It was difficult not to notice the heads that turned towards him. Clearly a natural reaction from the people he was around.

"I can see that. I think he came to see the medical director," I told her looking away from the door.

"I don't think so." I could hear the laughter in her voice again.

"Good evening, ladies."

"Hello Mr Essien," Nadia answered him with unbridled joy. "I loved the party at your mansion, the Christmas party. I hope I get to go again this year."

"Anything is possible," Aiden answered with one hand in his pocket. His beautiful eyes flashed in my direction.

"Hello," I said, puzzled by his presence in the hospital. Our parting had not been so smooth, and I figured that had been the end of our awkward relationship.

"I came to ask you to have dinner with me Simi."

"You do not waste any time, do you? Just straight to the point."

"I'd rather not waste your time."

"Why?" I tried not to sound rude.

"I'm sure after a long day of helping people you must be hungry."

I had to admit he had perfect timing on that part.

"She's hungry. She's only had breakfast," Nadia chimed in.

"Maybe I am, but what makes you think I would have dinner with you?"

I caught Nadia's gaping mouth. She looked positively stunned.

"I'm not so sure, but I'm here asking and hoping you would humour me."

"I can't leave my patients."

"I made a call your boss a few minutes ago, and he's approved of you taking the night off."

I was both flattered and angry at the same time.

"You can't go about doing that," I spat.

"Will you humour me? I won't take no for an answer," he continued as if he had not heard me.

"I'll have to make a quick call."

I dialled the Medical director's office number and was given a straightforward reply. 'Take the night off Nurse Simi'.

"It seems you've charmed your way into having me for company. I'll get my bag."

"Thank you."

He did not come with his driver that evening.

"Where are we going?"

"Somewhere nice," he responded with a bedazzling smile.

Cafe Claude was a high-end cosy restaurant in the heart of Orient City. Only the elite could afford to eat at such a place. Soft music played in the dimly lit room, and I felt a little embarrassed as I looked down on the sundress I was wearing. A waiter came around to usher us to our table after checking our reservation. I stared at the vase on the table, which held a single white lily to keep my eyes from roaming.

"What would you like to order?" Aiden asked, picking up the menu in front of him. He put it back on the table almost immediately.

I took up my menu and examined it.

"I think I'd like the stuffed chicken. I'm starving."

At the corner of my eye, I could see someone who looked a little bit like a famous soap opera actress. I soon realised it was her.

Another waiter came over, and he offered us another table away from prying eyes, but Aiden kindly declined. Soon after he left, the manager came over to ask us, no, pleaded with us to be placed next to the indoor fountain. To this, Aiden politely declined. The manager himself took my order and left. I was glad the theatrics were over.

"I'm sorry about all that," Aiden apologised. "It comes with the name."

"I understand." I smiled to put him at ease. Or was it to put me at ease? I already felt so out of place.

A different waiter walked to our table and handed Aiden a leather-bound book. He flipped it open and said a number. The waiter smiled and left. Soon after he was back with a bottle of wine and a plate of something bite-sized.

"Some amuse-bouche," he spoke directly to me.

"What is it?"

"Cheese and bacon stuffed mushrooms."

I tried some, and my taste buds came alive. Also, with the wine, I could have sworn I had gone to gourmet heaven. Aiden drank wine and said nothing. The main dish was brought in the finest of China, and I dug in.

"What?" You've never seen a woman eat before?" I inquired when I caught Aiden staring.

He replied, leaning over a little.

"That's not it."

"This isn't much of a dinner if you're not eating." There was no food item on his side of the table, save for a bottle of wine.

"I'll eat."

"If you say so."

He leaned back, crossing one leg over the other. He cleared his throat to jumpstart his words. He looked a bit uneasy.

"The flowers..." he began to say.

I cut him short. "You presumed they were for me."

"Yes."

"Yes, yes, they are."

"From anyone special?"

"Not that I know of," I replied with a quiet voice. "Are we going to talk about flowers or are you going to tell me the reason why I'm actually here?"

"More wine?" he offered.

"No, thank you."

"To the point then. Indeed there is an ulterior motive for you being here."

"Go ahead," I urged him.

"I know the last time we were together, there was a bit of tension between us and I acted poorly."

A bit?

"For that, I'm sorry. I truly am."

"You are forgiven."

"That was easy."

I shrugged and kept on eating.

"There'll be a fundraiser at The Phantom hotel the day after tomorrow for the renovation of the state's museum and for children with Down Syndrome. A simple event, nothing big. I want you to accompany me."

"I thought you rich people don't attend such events. Don't you usually send a lackey?"

"Not for this one I'm not. This one I want to attend."

"The day after tomorrow, that's Valentine's Day."

"It'll be a Fundraising slash Valentine's Day event."

"I've never been to The Phantom," I voiced under my breath. I was deep in thought for a few moments. Attending one of the elite's shindigs would be nice. It wasn't like I had any plans that day other than to eat junk food and watch anything I could find on cable.

"Why me Aiden Essien? Again. Why not some model? I'm sure you have a few on your speed dial."

"I know no model except the one that's sitting opposite me."

"Is that flattery I hear from you?"

"Apparently yes. I hope it works."

"Maybe if you try harder."

I ate a few forkfuls of my dinner.

"If I wanted some model, I would not be here, on the verge of begging. But here I am."

A faint tingling sensation crept up my arms.

"I'll come to pick you up at 7."

"I haven't even said yes."

"You did."

I cleaned my mouth with a napkin.

"You read minds now?"

"No, just your mind."

I gazed into his bright blue eyes, unable to make out his thoughts.

"I'll be waiting," I told him.

***

The next day when the doorbell rang, it was Henry who stood outside the door, a permanent scowl still etched to his face.

"Mr Essien asked me to bring you this," he said, handing me a carton covered package and a box with a pink bow on top. He turned around and left before I had the time to give a response.

I wasted no time in opening the carton. Inside it was the Ovo painting he had in his gallery. I smiled and laughed and smiled again, just staring at the picture. Remembering the box, I carefully removed the bow to reveal the contents. There was a strapless red dress, lush and soft and beneath it was an ankle strap pair of heels which I doubted would be seen under the flowing dress. There was a smaller box which held a necklace of intricate design. My mouth flew wide open by its sheer brilliance.

"These cannot be real diamonds, right?"

I peered at the necklace through and through.

"They can't right?" I asked myself and came up with the right answer. They were.

Later that afternoon at my sister's spa, I made sure I kept the reason for getting my hair and nails done to myself when she asked who I was looking beautiful for. She would blow things out of proportion if she knew the truth.

***

"I guess I was right again," Aiden said as I stepped out of my house. The time was 6:59pm. He was standing beside the white Hermès limousine. His hair had been neatly cut, and he was cleanly shaven. "You look stunning Simi."

"You look stunning too," I threw his compliment back at him as he adjusted his red cravat. He extended his hand, which I took. His touch made me light headed.

"As a great man once said, 'clothes don't make the man, but they go a long way toward making the businessman'."

My giggling welled.

He pulled me closer and said, "Words cannot describe how perfect you look tonight."

"You're getting good at this."

"What?"

"Flattery."

He gently let go of my hand. "You are beautiful Simi. It's about time someone told you."

"People do."

"As they should."

He opened the door to let me in.

When we settled in, he spoke into the car's intercom. "The Phantom Hotel, Wallace."

"Right away, sir," the chauffeur replied.

"You're not wearing it."

Aiden's gaze was directed at my bare chest.

I brought the necklace out of my Furla clutch purse.

"I'm sorry. I couldn't. It looks so goddamn expensive."

"So?"

"So I can't go strutting about with it."

"It belonged to my grandmother. My grandfather gave it to her on their thirtieth anniversary."

"That's exactly why I should not even dream about wearing it," I said trying to convince him

"She handed this to me, and now I'm giving it to you. I want you to have it."

Hearing him say that gave me shivers. Good ones.

"But..."

"No buts," he held his hand up to stop me from speaking any further. "Just say you'll wear the necklace."

There was a long unneeded pause because I already knew my answer.

"Okay. I'll wear it."

"Here, let me put it on for you."

His hands lingered on my bare skin, sending my thoughts into a state of unrest. A moan escaped from my lips, and he must have heard it because he chuckled slightly.

"Thank you," I told him, moving away from his reach, "for the painting too. It was generous of you."

"You probably love it more than I do. It deserves to be with someone like you."

Someone like me. What did that mean?

As soon as we got out of the car, the lights from the cameras flashed violently it almost blinded me.

Cameras. I had not expected them. It was foolish of me to have assumed it was an event that did not need media coverage. What were the words Aiden had used? Simple function. Nothing big.

Aiden seemed to have felt my uneasiness to which he said, "Smile Simi, I won't leave you."

I felt reassured and made an effort to smile.

Aiden took my arm in his and glided with me into the hotel. He did the gliding, and I did the tumbling and following.

The hall was nothing short of majestic. The columns on all sides of the room reminded me of another time and another place where magical things happened. The rose centrepieces were exquisite as well as the lights that dropped from the ceiling. As the party went on and the food and drinks flowed, performances were given by entertainers. When the Governor finally showed with his beautiful wife and entourage, a virtual tour of the new museum was given, and some of the artworks were showcased.

"Are you enjoying yourself?" Aiden asked as a slideshow presentation went on.

"A bit. It's enlightening," I replied, giving a half smile.

After a long speech by the president of the National Down Syndrome Society and a presentation by a renowned developmental paediatrician, the MC announced that it was time to let go of the fundraising spirit and take up the Valentine's Day spirit before donations began. A song came on which got most of the attendees reaching for their partners.

"Will the gentlemen please take their special ladies to the dance floor?" The MC's voice floated over from the speakers.

Aiden eased from his seat, offering his hand, and I shrunk back.

"I'm your special lady?"

"I'm standing here, aren't I?"

"I can't dance to this. I'm more of an erratic sort of dancer." My words came out all hurried and disoriented.

"I'll lead, just follow."

"Are you…"

"Just come with me and stop complaining."

Aiden's left arm wound around my body. He held my right hand in his left and my stomach knotted in response. We rocked from side to side to the rhythm of the slow song. I caught a few eyes gawking at us and a few exchanges of words between three ladies.

"This is so weird, Aiden. I've never done this before. I think I'm going to step on your shoes."

"You won't. And if you do, I'll pretend you didn't."

His retorting smirk made me want to punch him.

"This is just an excuse to be closer to you. You should know that by now."

"Are you always this honest, Mr Essien?"

"Sometimes, Miss Oladeji. The truth can be a powerful weapon when used properly."

"And what is the reason for all this? The truth, if you don't mind."

He twirled me around and said nothing. He pulled me even closer to his rigid body and buried his head on my neck. Feeling his warm breath against my skin filled my head with all sorts of crazy thoughts. He was so easy to be with. I felt lighter than the air just by being close to him.

"Simi," he murmured, lifting his head from my shoulders to let his gaze fall upon my lips. A devastating effect on me. For that single moment, the entire world ceased to exist.

"Aiden."

His gaze did not falter.

"The music has stopped."

A smile slowly crept up to his face as he moved back and took a half bow.

"Oh, I was getting worn-out anyway," I mumbled quickly to hide my anxiety. We were back in our seats in a few strides and back to sipping wine and eating finger foods.

Aiden scowled from his wine glass. I turned around to see the woman he was glaring at.

He said, "I was going to ask you to dance with me again, but I have to deal with this."

"Aiden sweetheart you look handsome. Just like your father."

"Emmeline, how long have you been here?"

"Don't think me a fool Aiden, I know you spotted me a while ago and ignored me."

"Emmeline this is Simi Oladeji, Simi, this is Emmeline Zimmerman, my mother's best friend and spy."

I stared in awe of the woman who took on a defensive stance. Her lips twitched as she stared down at Aiden. She was a rather tall woman with high cheekbones that suited her face. Her brown eyes spoke of a time when she was once the belle of the ball. The grey hair added a tinge of allure to her brown hair.

"It's nice to meet you," I said to her.

"Oh, nonsense. Spy?" she asked as if she had just been accused of a heinous crime and completely ignoring me in the process. I may as well have been another chair. She said something in German in a high pitched voice. Aiden replied her, his baritone becoming more pronounced. This went on for a full minute.

"Then what are you doing here?"

They were back to English again.

"I just came to see how you were doing."

"On behalf of my mother, I'm sure."

"Naturally."

Aiden laughed, but it was not the same laughter I was used to that could be seen in his eyes. This one was different. It was mocking laughter.

"How long has it been since you talked to your mother?"

"Two years and counting."

"It's unlike you to be away for this long."

"Unlike me? Then why isn't she here to say that herself?"

The woman remained quiet. She glared at me and said "I know that necklace. That's The Starlight. How did you get it?"

She did not need to wait for my answer before she figured it out for herself. She transferred her gaze from me to Aiden. "It's been worn by better."

"Emmeline, keep your thoughts to yourself," Aiden told her sternly.

"I think I'll leave now. I've seen all that is needed."

She left without looking back.

"I'm sorry about that," Aiden apologised.

"It's alright. People have the right to talk bad about me or insult me, but it doesn't mean I have bend over backwards to please them."

"I like your philosophy."

I waited before asking. "Is it true? About your mother."

"Afraid so. We have a complicated relationship," he told me massaging the back of his neck. I pressed the issue no further.

"How much are you worth?"

"How much does Forbes say I'm worth?"

"I don't go about researching you remember?"

"Not enough money, I'm afraid."

My eyes dilated unconsciously.

"You see, when my father started his business, he asked himself that if he wanted to make money, why not just become one of the world's richest men?"

"It's one way to get motivated."

"Uh, huh."

"Is it true your grandfather was one of the richest men in Germany?"

"I thought you didn't go about researching me."

I nearly choked on my drink.

"I just stumbled upon the information."

"He was."

"Did your father marry your mother for the money?" I wanted to take the words back, but they were already out there. "I'm sorry," I said. "I didn't mean it that way."

"It's alright. Part of it is true. When my father married my mother, his assets skyrocketed. He was able to gain favours from investors and business associates of my grandfather's. But one thing I knew for sure was that he loved her. And she did too. Maybe even more than he loved her."

"Well, you're lucky, being born into wealth."

"Lucky you say. Getting the money is a strenuous load of work, but making more money and keeping it takes thrice the work. I'm responsible for more than a thousand people who need me on my A game at all times to have a job. I cannot afford mistakes."

He rubbed his temple and took for himself another drink from the passing waiters. Something about the way he said responsible warmed my heart. He looked like a father talking about his children.

"Oh my god," I yelped.

"What?" Aiden asked, looking around as if in anticipation of an attack.

"That's Bianca Grace," I revealed in a hushed whisper.

Aiden turned his head towards the direction I was pointing.

"Yes, CEO of Orbit magazine. I've never seen a more violent person."

"You know her?" I asked wide-eyed.

"I've met her a few times."

"She's just as pretty as she is in her magazine. No one would believe she's over 40."

A thought came to me. Without my sister, I would never have known Bianca Grace, the eclectic, beautiful woman whose magazine featured mostly beauty houses. Once a spa gets featured in her magazine, the next day finds the stars and the wealthy folks alike trooping into it.

I began, "I was wondering... um. Never mind."

"What is it, Simi?"

"It's nothing."

"Not asking won't get you what you want."

"I was just overwhelmed by seeing her."

"I can get you to meet her if you want."

I politely declined.

Aiden studied me for a while before saying, "if you say so, Simi."

"But you can arrange my meeting with him."

The lights flooded the stage where Teju stood.

"I've never met anyone who doesn't like him!"

Aiden had to speak louder because of the screams that erupted from the guests. Teju simply looked down and winked in response to the crowd. This only resulted in more screams.

"My nieces adore him. I have to get a picture with him."

After his performance, I was able to get several pictures with the sensational superstar, with Aiden's help of course. He was in a hurry to leave for another show, but Aiden was able to convince him otherwise.

Scrolling through the pictures in my phone, I said to Aiden, who was standing in front of me "my sister is going to flip over on her backside when she sees this."

"I'm happy you're happy," Aiden lips curved into a smile.

I stared back at him, frozen by the lights reflected off his eyes. He narrowed them slightly.

"I have to meet a few people. I'll meet you back at our table."

"Okay."

I watched him move through the cluster of tables and noticed a man in dark blue tuxedo move towards an older man. I had caught a glimpse of him while posing for the camera with Teju who, by the way, was a total sweetheart. His shifty eyes and movements had caught my attention, but I had given no thought to it. Now, he was moving stealthily toward the man and brought something out from his pocket. I looked around for any security personnel, but there was none. I clearly saw the object as the light fell on it.

I ran to him.

"Hey, what are you, stop…"

I spurned him around and at the same time stopped on my tracks.

The bulging teary eyes of the unknown man made me realise what had just happened. My falling body was caught by a table. We crashed together, wine spilling all over my face. There was a loud scream from someone, others accompanied hers soon enough. The pain hit me hard and fast.

"Simi!" I heard Aiden's voice. "I leave you for a moment, and you get yourself shot," he said in exasperation, holding me up.

"Someone call an ambulance." A man bawled.

"No time," Aiden spoke in a voice not belonging to him.

I winced, and tears came pouring down my cheeks when he lifted me up.

"Aiden it hurts."

I knew the bullet must have pierced a vital organ or two. I coughed, and blood spewed out of my mouth like it was meant to.

"I'm here. I won't let anything happen to you. I promise." His tone was firm and assuring. He lifted me into his arms and soon I could smell the confines of a car.

"Aiden…" I called softly. The pain was too much. I could feel my consciousness seeping away. Was death approaching? My heart raced, and my breath quickened. I was too young to die. My dress was soaked with so much blood I felt sorry for it.

"Drink this." He told me in a harsh voice.

"What..?"

I looked up to Aiden's face. He did not look at himself. His hair looked much whiter, and his eyes looked like glowing embers.

"Drink dammit!" he bawled, offering me his hand, which he placed on my quivering lips.

I tasted blood.

Who's ever heard of a blood transfusion through the mouth? I wanted to refuse it, but I felt myself swallowing the metallic tasting liquid. Strangely, the pain lessened gradually until I could barely feel it.

"Aiden I …"

He shushed me, and to my relief, I saw a smile on his worried face.

"Sleep now."

CHAPTER 7

It was the second time I was waking up in an unfamiliar bed, but this time Aiden was by my side, his blue eyes I could tell had been keenly watching over me.

"Don't move too much," he warned.

"You…"

"Don't say anything. You lost a lot of blood."

"What did you…?"

"Shush. You should eat something to get your strength back."

"Don't shush me. I don't need food. I need answers."

A piercing pain shot up in my chest but soon disappeared

"I had a feeling you would say that."

When he moved closer with his chair, I edged back on the bed.

"Don't be scared. I won't hurt you."

"I drank something. Your blood? I was shot." I was confused.

"Yes you were, but you're better now,"

"What did you do? What are you?"

My question caused his expression to change. His hands balled into fists.

"I'm nothing you should be afraid of."

"You keep saying I should not be scared, but you haven't told me anything. What are you? Tell me!"

"I can't."

"Then I shouldn't be here."

I made to stand up.

"Simi don't go."

"Then you sure as hell better start talking. I know what happened that night when I was attacked by those hooligans and what happened at the party."

He sprang to his feet and paced about. He ran a hand through his hair and exhaled loudly.

At last, he said something.

"I would put it in two words you can understand; shape-shifter."

The words sounded both familiar and mysterious at the same time.

"You're a shape-shifter? Like you can transform into different things?"

"Just one thing."

"That's ridiculous."

"I won't lie to you about this."

"I'm so confused."

"That night, when you were attacked, what did you see?"

I was glad to know I had not made up things in my head, but it was not the time to gloat.

"I don't know what I saw. I just heard the growls of an animal I think. Now that I think about it, I'm sure I heard it. It had to be a gigantic version of an animal. A lion, tiger maybe. Those men were terrified of it." I paused. "That was you?"

He buried his head in his hands and groaned as if in pain.

"But how? And you healed me, how?"

He came back to the bed.

"When I first saw you, I knew there was something about you. I did not know how I knew you were in trouble and why I was able to see you. Clear as day. I got angry enough to want to kill those bastards and ... I just know I was able to do what I had never done before."

His words made no sense to me.

"How did you become part beast and part human?"

"So you believe me?"

"I see no reason why you should make this up."

"I guess that's one way to judge the situation."

"Yes, go on."

"At first, I did not know what I was, but after literally going back to my roots, I was able to put things together. This research took a chunk of my time and a lot of resources."

I hugged the blanket.

"The first time I ever shifted, turned, transformed, was in my grandfather's estate in Ireland. I had gone there during my school break. Charlotte had flown in from Berlin with my mother to see me then."

"Who's Charlotte?"

"She is the daughter of Emmeline and was my closest friend."

"Was?"

"After everything that I'm about to tell you which she witnessed first-hand, we grew apart. We still exchange pleasantries, but it gets so awkward. She did not loathe me, unlike some people. No, she was just afraid of me."

There was no doubting the pain in his voice as he spoke.

"I remember I was in the atrium with my mother and grandmother and I cannot remember what triggered it, an argument maybe but all I knew was, I lost myself and became what I am today. I transformed into a 'scary monster'. When I came to, I learned that my other half had run into the stables and killed most of the horses and had left a big scar on my mother's neck. It was a miracle *it*—I—did not kill my mother. The man in charge of the horses had used a tranquilliser to put me down and chained me up. No one knew what I was." Aiden struggled with his words.

"What happened after?"

"I became very sick. Everyone thought I was going to die. I was homeschooled until I had to leave for business school. My mother became terrified of me. She did not bother to hide it, and her scar reminded me of what I was."

That certainly explained his complicated relationship with his mother.

"My grandmother, on the other hand, was very supportive. To her, I was still her little boy and nothing else. I wanted to know more about what happened, so I decided to make an effort to shape-shift, but I made sure to do it while chained in the underground room of the house in Ireland. I used a lot of methods, and I'm ashamed to say this, but I actually tried transforming on a full moon thinking I was a werewolf. None of these helped, but I kept on trying. It wasn't until I felt the insane need to hunt something down and kill it was I able to transform. For 12 hours, I was completely out of my body. Thanks to the chains and a solid door, the creature was unable to roam free."

"This is beginning to sound like something out of a bizarre horror movie."

"I assure you all these things are true and I'm letting you know because I never want you to be afraid of me and I think you deserve to know."

"I... I....." my voice trailed off.

He blinked twice and asked, "Do you want me to continue?"

"Y...yes."

"Are you sure?"

"I really do. I want to know everything. Like how did you know about your blood being able to do what it does?"

"I scraped a knee. When I looked back on the wound, it wasn't there. At first, I was scared out of my mind, but I went straight to the kitchen, got a knife and cut myself. In a matter of seconds, I was healed, no scar, nothing. So I conducted a little experiment with Henry? I figured if I could heal myself, then I could heal others."

"Henry?"

"Yes, he was the one who shot me with the tranquilliser."

"And he let you?"

"Yes, Henry has always been loyal to my family and me and really quite protective. He has worked for my family for three decades. ."

"Oh."

Now I understood why he was not very eager to have me around.

'How many know you're a..."

"My mother, grandmother, Henry and Charlotte.

"And your father and grandfather?"

He shook his head. "My grandmother swore everyone to secrecy. She was a very persuasive woman."

"But how did you come to be this way?"

"I had to draw up theories, most of which were inconclusive, but the only theory that came out right was genetics, I had experts look into my family history. Both my families. Although, my father's history proved rather difficult to ascertain with not much record keeping to look into. My great great great grandmother Abigail Gunther came to Nigeria in the 1800s to see the Old Oyo Empire. When she got back, she said she had been bitten by a werewolf, but no one believed her. They said the jungle fever had gotten to her."

He paused and then resumed talking.

"I got most of my information about my father's family through word of mouth, but nothing worth knowing about my nature came out of it. It was not until I learned about the old Yoruba myths and legends from an Ifa priest who had great knowledge about them that I got headway. He told me an old Yoruba legend of a clan called Meje whose people had been cursed by an old wizard they had sentenced to death. The wizard had told the Meje clan that since they were so bloodthirsty, they would be bloodthirsty forever. You see, the rest of the clan blamed this wizard as the cause of all their problems and thought killing him would end it all."

"That seems a bit harsh," I stated.

"Yes, it was."

"What happened to the Meje people?"

"They disappeared."

"What?"

"Either they vanished and went to the spirit world and or they were killed. All of them."

"What do you think? Do you think you are one of them?"

"I don't know. I'm yet to deduce that."

"Aiden."

"Yes?"

He moved closer to me, but this time, I did not shrink back.

"I need water. I'm thirsty."

He called on Edna who brought a glass of water in a tray.

"Thank you," I told her.

She winked at me before she left.

"Does she know?" I asked, the water in the glass all gone.

"No. She would never understand. You see the curse made the Meje people bloodthirsty beasts. I know this because I've felt it. I've felt it ever since the first time I killed those horses. At first, I did not transform very much, but when I hit my early twenties, the hunger got worse, and even though I try to curb it, it just keeps growing. It's why I chain myself up whenever I feel the urge. In the room, you nearly wandered into. In the library."

I realised why he did not want me snooping.

"So you won't have to harm anyone."

"Yes. At that time, I can't control it no matter how I try. The pain of shifting is unbearable. Every cell in my body feels like it's boiling but killing something, anything brings a certain type of satisfaction."

"So it does hurt when you transform I mean."

"It's the most painful thing you can imagine."

I studied the rise and fall of his chest as his breathing steadied. I was in deep thought for a while, and so was he.

"I have so much information to sift through I don't know where to begin."

"Take your time."

"How were you able to sense I was in trouble??"

He replied, "I don't know. I was in control of myself for the first time. I didn't harm those men because of the thrill of the hunt. I hurt them because they hurt you. Well, hurt them, is a gentle way of putting it. The thing is, I was fully in control and not at all uneasy."

"But you changed knowing you would be in pain."

"I had to save you. You would have died."

"This is all too strange."

"I know."

He took my hand in his, and I let him.

"Wait a minute. If I drank your blood, does that mean..."

"No," he smiled. "No, you won't be like me."

He laughed when I let out a sigh of relief.

"Now that you know the truth, you should stay away from me. It'll be the most logical thing to do. I'll understand."

I wanted to hug him and tell him I was not going anywhere even if he was a mad beast or monster. Also, I tried to get the hell out of the house as fast as my legs could carry me, but instead I said, "no you idiot. You saved my life twice, and if you wanted to kill me, I'm sure you would have done that a long time ago."

What have I gotten myself into?

He clearly was not fully human, yet I could not bring myself to flee and looking at him, he had never looked more vulnerable, more human. He had shared with me his greatest secret, after all.

"The man who had the knife..." I began to ask to derail my train of thoughts.

"He just got out of jail and was out to get some revenge on the Judge who sent him there in the first place. Now he's back there for life. The man whose life you saved was Judge Abuchi's."

"I'm glad."

"I'm not. It was honourable what you did going after him, but you could have died."

"But here I am alive and well."

He reassuringly squeezed my hand.

"Need I ask what day it is?"

"Monday."

I had been asleep for three days.

"I'm sure everyone would be out looking for the girl who saved the Judge."

"You've become quite famous. But the first thing you should do is see your sister. Big sister syndrome."

***

It was already past noon when I arrived at Ava's house the next day. I was nearly toppled over by her hug.

"We heard what happened. Are you okay?"

"I'm fine now. Aiden took care of me. Where's your husband?"

"Out. You never told me you were going out with Aiden Essien."

"I'm not going out with Aiden," I objected.

"Then what's this?" she said shoving a copy of Elite! in my face. The front page of the magazine had a picture of me and Aiden walking hand in hand into the Phantom hotel.

"There are three pages of your pictures together."

"Why would, why would they do that?" I was on the verge of hyperventilating.

"When the most eligible bachelor in the country, nay, Africa, gets snatched up, everyone in ought to know."

"He's not snatched. He hasn't been snatched up. He's still a bachelor. Those ladies shouldn't have to worry."

"And this?" she pointed out a picture where Aiden and I were dancing. "He looks really interested in you from what I see."

"When did they? No."

"Yes."

"Really?"

My sister laughed, shaking her head.

"Your nieces have been sending the pictures to all their friends. I don't think I've ever seen them so happy."

"You probably want to see this."

I gave her my phone.

"You met Teju! Of course, you did."

"Oh yeah."

"I'm so jealous. How was he?"

"He's adorable."

She brought out her new phone.

'Oh, I knew that already. I can tell. He has that face. I can't wait to show the girls."

I became quite popular at the hospital after the incident. Those who never talked to me started having long conversations with me, which I hated. A radio and television station and a magazine wanted to do an interview with me. I declined their offer.

I tried not to over-think about Aiden and his life. It only gave me a headache and spurned more questions. Could magic really exist? Or werewolves or shape-shifters and what if all Aiden had told me actually happened a long time ago? Were curses really effective? It was challenging to doubt Aiden's story. He was proof of it. I was proof of it.

"Simi Oladeji?" A woman called my name from the small doorway, which led to the pharmacy.

"Yes, that's me."

The small woman gave a toothy smile. She was most likely in her late 50s.

"I heard you were back. Can we talk somewhere else? I don't feel so comfortable in hospitals."

"Sure."

I led her to the cafeteria, and we sat next to the large painting of a house by a lake.

"My name is Merit Abuchi. I'm sure you know my husband."

"Yes, I do."

"My husband would have been here with me today, but he was called away. He sent me on his behalf. He's so grateful, and he wants you to know the man who was after his life has been locked up. What you did was..." she stopped talking to clean her teary eyes with a pink hanky. "And you were shot. That bullet was meant for my husband, but you stopped it to your own detriment. Are you alright, now?"

"Yes, ma. I'm fine."

"Who paid your hospital bills? No one could locate you after the incident."

"I paid the bills."

The truth would more than likely give her a cardiac myopathy.

"Then I must reimburse you. I have to find a way to thank you."

"A simple thank you would suffice. I cannot accept your money."

"Oh the humility and ..."

She was on the verge of tears again. Anyone could tell she was a very emotional woman.

She dried her eyes and spoke firmly. "If you ever need anything, I mean anything; don't hesitate to come to me. Here's my card."

"Well, I do have something you can help me with."

I told her about the hospital's foundation and how her donations were welcomed. She wasted no time in writing a cheque.

"Thank you."

"Don't thank me, dear. I should be thanking you."

I had good reason to be grateful. Without that incident, I may never have known about Aiden and his secret. I may never have felt closer to him.

Later that day, I was surprised to find a man and two little girls no more than six years old on my front door.

"I'm Martin Abuchi."

"Hello."

"My mother told me all that happened today. I know you won't take money or anything from us, but you have my sincere gratitude. You gave me back, my father and my daughters, their grandfather."

The two girls struggled to get free from their father, but he held them tight.

"Just accept this if you won't take anything else."

He signalled the two men who were standing close to the two posh BMWs, and soon they began bringing gift baskets from the cars and placed them to my feet. There was seven pretty gift baskets total. I thanked him for the baskets after which he too gave me his card.

Femi drove by a few minutes after the man and his family left.

"Detective Femi," I hailed.

He wrapped his arms around me before saying, 'I cannot believe you would do something so reckless."

"I am fine. Fit as a fiddle."

"Simi, I would have been here sooner, but I was on an assignment."

He let go of me. I ushered him inside and closed the door behind him.

"Have you had lunch yet?" I inquired.

He replied, slumping down on a couch, "no, not yet, but I'm not here to eat, I'm here because of what happened to you."

"What happened?"

I took a carrot from my fridge to nibble on.

"This Aiden Essien fellow. The first time you went to his house, you got sick, and then you got mortally wounded at another party with him."

"People get shot all the time, no big deal."

"No, they don't. They get headaches and colds. Maybe you should not be hanging around him so much."

"Maybe I should not be hanging around you so much," I told him jokingly.

"I'm serious. Something about him is just off."

My chest tightened.

"Nothing about him is off."

"Just be careful, and don't go about putting yourself in danger. I have seen a lot of bad things, and I don't want anything bad to happen to you."

"I will, now relax let me get you something to eat."
"What's with all the gift baskets?"
"Benefits of getting shot," I answered laughing.

CHAPTER 8

Ava called me out of work for something she could not tell me over the phone. All she had to say was that I needed to be at her spa pronto, and the surprise would blow my head off. I had half the mind not to go because I wanted to keep my head. I told her I would be there in an hour because I had to sign out of the hospital.

Her spa was occupied with unfamiliar people carrying cameras when I arrived. Also, the girls working for her looked extra pretty. I had never seen my sister look so drop dead beautiful before. Her curly weave was parted midway, and the maxi dress she had on did well to accentuate her curves. She was talking to another woman in suit trousers and a fitted jacket. She saw me and waved me over.

"What's happening here?"

"Simi, this is Tammy Charles. Tammy is from Orbit, and she's here to do a feature on my spa. Ah!" Her excited scream filled the waiting room. "I wanted to surprise you, so when they called yesterday, I kept my mouth shut. You have no idea how difficult it was for me. I don't know how this happened, but I'm so glad it is happening."

The woman left us to talk.

"Miss Charles said someone referred them here. Someone who was able to get her boss to redirect them from another spa to come here today."

"I think I know who's behind all this."

"Who?"

"At the party, I mentioned it, well not mentioned, to Aiden. I'm sure he set up all these."

"Then we have to thank him. But all of that will have to wait."

She started scrutinising my entire body.

"No, this won't do."

"What?"

"Your outfit."

I looked down on my t-shirt and cotton trousers with brown suspenders.

"I look chic."

"You need a dress."

"Odes," she called one of the girls. "Get my sister a dress, will you?"

"You sell clothes in your spa now?"

"That's a good business idea. You'll be my first customer."

Over the next few days, I tried to contact Aiden, but he was nowhere to be found. I wondered if our conversation had anything to do with it. I should be the one running, not him.

Nadia could tell something was wrong and asked, but I refused to share. About a week later, he showed up at the hospital after I gave up trying to get hold of him.

"I knew it!" Nadia voiced in a hushed tone. "I knew it. You should have seen your face just now when he walked in. Lit up like a Christmas tree."

I shooed her away and waited for Aiden to reach the table I had shared with Nadia in the cafeteria. He said his hello to her and sat beside me.

"Henry told me you came to see me."

Something about him felt different.

"What happened? You went off the grid for a while."

"I was...um....busy."

"Busy?"

"Yes. Missed me?"

"Don't get cocky. I know what you did."

"I've done a lot of things. You have to remind me which sin."

"You talked to Bianca Grace, didn't you? They were at my sister's spa a few days ago doing what they do best."

"Was she happy, your sister?"

"Delighted."

"Were you happy?"

"Delighted as well."

"I hoped you would be. You know you should not keep things to yourself."

"What can I do to repay such generosity?" I asked, folding my arms.

"You can come away with me for the weekend."

"Why would I do that?"

"Cause you missed me. I am flying out to see some folks in Calabar, and I want you to come with me."

"This weekend?"

"Yes, and I know you have no excuse not to come. You have this weekend and next week off."

"Have you been spying on me?"

'No," he said plainly, "I just have perfect timing. I need it to get what I want."

"And if I say I don't want to go with you?"

"Then we'll try a different approach, maybe blackmail."

"Okay," I conceded. "I'll go with you."

"We'll have fun. I promise you. Maybe not the type of fun you're used to, but we'll have fun."

"Simi!"

I turned to see the source of the voice. It was Femi. He took decisive steps in approaching us. Aiden stood up immediately.

"Femi this is…"

"I know who he is. Aiden Essien."

I watched the two of them size each other up. It was pathetic to watch.

"Femi um...I did not catch your last name."

"Bamidele"

"I don't know any Bamidele."

Aiden's blue eyes became darker, or maybe it was just my imagination.

"You wouldn't."

I had never felt so much tension in so small a space.

"Well, it was nice meeting you Femi. Simi, I'll pick you up Friday by two. Pack light."

'Sure thing."

Femi replaced Aiden on the chair. I could smell, see, taste and feel the disapproval exuding from Femi's composure.

"What's happening on Friday?"

"Nothing."

"Stay away from him Simi."

I was taken aback by the way the order came from him.

"You can't tell me what and what not to do."

His face eased a little from its fierceness.

"Sorry, just be careful around him."

Why he was so cautious of Aiden bothered me. This was beyond ugly jealousy. I could tell.

"Why are you here, Femi?"

"I helped a family retrieve their stolen heirloom, and they've given me a temporary membership card to the city's country club. I thought we could go down there this weekend and play some tennis, or golf whichever takes your interest."

"Uh..." The reply to his offer got stuck in my throat. I cleared it several times before speaking. "Femi I'm sorry, but I don't think I'll be able to go with you."

"Does it have anything to do with Mr Fancy?"

"Aiden," I corrected. "Yes, I already agreed to do something with him."

'What?" Femi probed, his countenance slowly changing.

"Something important."

He made to leave.

I quickly added, "But we can go next weekend, can't we?"

He pondered on my offer for a while. His answer was short and brusque. "Yes, we can."

"Then next weekend it is. Let me walk you downstairs."

"Thanks, I can find my way."

I could see the disappointment he felt weigh heavy on him, but there was nothing I could do to prevent it.

***

I had no idea where we were headed in Calabar. By noon on Friday, I had on a purple Jalabiya, rope-on sandals and carried a small duffel bag. Aiden came by sporting a yellow blazer on a white shirt and blue jeans. His hair was all jumbled up like he just stepped out of bed. I loved the look.

"You look like an Arabian princess," was his only comment.

"Where are we going, Aiden?" I asked him for the nth time as we boarded the plane.

"Cross River State."

"I know. But where in its capital?"

"You'll see."

That was the same answer he had given to me the last time I asked. I was in for a surprise, and I could not wait to know. I hated not knowing. It irked me.

When we got to the airport in Calabar it was a few minutes past four, there was a car waiting to take us to our destination. As we passed the stadium, I recalled the last time I was there for the Christmas carnival.

That was five years ago, and the city had been packed full with people and the streets blocked. My phone was stolen that day.

The car slowed down as it branched off the main road and into a street lined on both sides by flowering trees. The vehicle gradually came to a halt in front of a building whose imposing gate had the inscription 'St. Thomas Orphanage.'

I turned to Aiden, who had a sly smile on his beautiful face. No amount of guesses prepared me for an orphanage.

"We are staying here for the weekend?"

"Yes."

"Are we on one of your philanthropic works?"

"Sorta."

His vague answer left me speechless. The gate opened up, and we drove in. My first take on the place was that it looked really homey and more comfortable than most orphanages I had seen. It was a three storey building painted grey with other smaller buildings behind it. The sound of children on the playground could be heard. One of the boys riding down the path expertly on a bike almost hit the car.

As we got out, one of the children shouted: "Uncle Aiden is here!"

Uncle Aiden?

I threw a questioning look at Aiden. He just shrugged.

There was an unending supply of hugs for him, and then the chattering started. One by one, they dished out the happenings of the previous year to him. Aiden surveyed the crowd and asked, "Where's Adam?"

"He was adopted yesterday," the tallest boy among them replied.

"That's amazing news."

"Who's the lady?" One of the little girls in a wheelchair asked.

"A friend."

The boy with the bike came up to me, his bike thrown haphazardly on the grass. He was no older than nine I predicted, but his dark eyes made him look mature.

"I'm Chidi. What's your name?"

"Simi." I chuckled at his air of forced confidence. "You look like an Arabian princess."

"Thank you." I gave Aiden a knowing look.

A girl no more than three with thin braids tugged at my dress and opened up her arms. I lifted her up and asked, "And what's your name, little princess?"

She giggled and hid her face on my shoulder.

"Her name is Rose, like the flower," Chidi replied. "Do you have any luggage? I can help you take it in."

Before I could reply a thin woman with a lengthy mass of grey hair and smoky eyes walked toward us as fast as her age would let her. Beside her were an average-looking man and another woman who looked just like her. The old woman threw her arms around Aiden and spoke rapidly to him. They began speaking a language I understood to be Efik. I heard the name Adam, which meant they were talking about the adopted boy.

"And who's this beautiful lady?" she asked in English.

"My friend."

"Yes, his friend," I repeated, not knowing why. "It's a pleasure to meet you."

"Aiden did not tell me he was bringing a friend over."

"I'm sure he didn't."

"You're most welcome."

Aiden informed me as we settled in that the older woman whose name was Mrs Akpan, the pioneer of the establishment and the other woman, Amaeka was her granddaughter. She was married to the man, Abraham Afiah, and both of them were the central staff in the orphanage. There were two other men and a woman who assisted them on occasion.

"I didn't know you could speak Efik."

"I had to learn from my father."

It was such minor information compared to my knowledge that he could shape-shift into an unknown creature when he was bloodthirsty.

"Well, now, you do."

I was shown my room on the third floor by Amaeka. She took Rose from me who was now sleeping and drooling on my dress. A few minutes ago, when I tried to put her down, she had clawed her way back to my shoulders and hung up there. Chidi found a way to get to my bag and brought it in himself. He placed it on the king sized bed and said as he backed out of the room "If you need anything, just come to me."

"I will thank you."

I chuckled when he winked.

The room was pleasant and smelled sweet. The pink walls matched the window blinds, and shelf of old books lined the wall. After my bath, I threw on an off white t-shirt and high waist plaid trousers and took a walk around the house. I passed by the kitchen to find Mrs Akpan and her daughter making a cake.

"Can I help?" I inquired taking a few steps forward.

"An extra hand is always welcome."

"Who's the cake for? One of the children?"

"It's for Aiden."

My unhinged jaw told them everything. Mrs Akpan laughed, her wrinkled forehead creasing terribly.

"He brings you here without warning, and then forgets to tell you tomorrow is his birthday. That boy is full of surprises, just like his father." Her statement made me realise that the orphanage was unique.

"Can you excuse me for just one minute? I'll be right back."

"Take your time, dear."

I went in search of Aiden and found him in the spacious sitting room. So many things were out of place, and the children talked incessantly. I was surprised to see him in a grey, and orange sweater with a duck splashed across the chest. His light blue slacks had whale patterns running down the entire length. He was playing a football game with Chidi on the big screen. After seeing the children, twenty in all, the only persons older than Chidi were the twins Taiye and Kehinde, a boy and a girl both twelve years old.

'You've reverted to a child," was the first thing that came out of my mouth.

The game was paused.

"Princess," Chidi said, dropping the gamepad. He took my hand, dragged me to a futon. There was little I could do to resist.

"So, what do you do Princess?"

I temporarily forgot I was there for Aiden.

"I'm a nurse."

"Awesome. You take care of sick people, right?"

"Yes, I do. Among other things."

"Maybe I should be a nurse too when I grow up."

"It's not a very easy job. You should get prepared."

"But you're a nurse, are you not?"

"I am."

"Then I can be too."

I smiled and rubbed his head.

"Just keep thinking that way, Chidi, and you will do great things."

"Awesome."

"Now I have to talk to Uncle Aiden, in private."

"Okay, but come back soon, Princess. I want you to see me play."

"I promise."

Aiden was by my side in a moment. We wandered out into the cold night and sat on the swings in the playground.

"He has certainly taken a shine to you."

"I can't stop a boy from having a crush on me now can I?"

"Chidi? No. He'll do whatever he wants."

"Why didn't you tell me about tomorrow?"

"I wanted to surprise you."

"A job well done. But it poses a problem. I have no gift for you."

"Don't worry, you can get me one and give it to me anytime. I'm not going anywhere."

"Now that poses another problem. What do I get a billionaire?"

He laughed. "I'm sure you'll think of something."

His eyes conveyed a feeling I could not comprehend. He moved his hand slowly on the rail and then stared into the night sky. It was cloudy, and the moon's beam was cut off almost completely.

"My father was raised here," he began to say. "He was left here by his father when he was just a baby. Mrs Akpan knew who he was. She knew he was too poor to take care of a baby whose mother had died during childbirth. She had no choice but to accept my father. Back then, this place was not an orphanage." He paused and then laughed as if someone had just told him a not so funny joke.

"My father brought me here when I was five, and when I saw the children living here, I knew I had to be grateful for what I had. My father did not have the same things I had growing up or lived in the same kind of buildings I lived in. He knew what it was to be poor and I didn't and probably never will. And when I met Mrs Akpan, it was like meeting my father's mother." His smiled dimmed but did not disappear. "I started coming here every year for my birthday since the time I took over my father's company."

"I can tell everyone loves having you here, especially the children."

He was on his feet in one swift motion. Going behind me, he gently pushed the swing, and my legs went off the ground.

"How old will you be tomorrow?"

"Older than you."

I laughed, and he did too. I wanted to turn around to see his face, but I stopped midway.

"I'll be thirty-one."

"Not that older. Just three years. That's barely any time."

His hands stopped the swing, and I could hear him take a deep breath behind me. "I was not busy with work by the way. I was trying not to break out of my chains and go on a killing spree."

My heart skipped a beat. I stood up uneasily while he walked to stand in front of me.

"You should have called me."

His eyes softened.

"I didn't want you to see me that way. So out of control and in so much pain."

I reached for him and enclosed him in my arms. His hands slowly wrapped around my waist.

"I'm glad you're okay," I said.

His warm breath caressed the back of my neck. I held him tight, not ever wanting to let go. He pulled me even close, and my feet nearly went off the ground.

"Dinner is almost ready!" someone said from the central doorway.

"I guess we better go in," he said, still holding me.

"Yes," I said and pulled away from him.

We had pizza for dinner. Apparently, it was a tradition for them to eat junk food whenever Aiden dropped by for his birthday.

The next day we had cookies, toast and mango juice for breakfast. The situation was incorrigible, but I could do nothing to stop it. Aiden asked the children where they wanted to go. Some said they wanted to see three new animation movies that were premiering and others wanted to go to the Alia water Park. After a bit of arguing and name calling, we decided to go to both places. We'd see only one movie first and then visit the Park later. Amaeka and her husband were to accompany us and keep an eye on the children. Mrs Akpan was too tired to move around with us young folks. Her exact words. It was all decided, and we all trooped into the double-decker bus which Aiden drove. Amaeka and her husband followed us with their Peugeot.

The movie started by 10 and lasted for two hours and by the time we were done, the children were all psyched to go to the park. As soon as we arrived at the park, the children changed into bathing suits. Rose, who had been with me the entire time let go off me when she saw the wave pool for children her age.

"Why are you still in that?" he pointed at my jeans.

Aiden was in bright red and white polka-dot shorts. His well-sculpted abs brought a sigh to my lips.

"I have nothing to change into."

"You never told me." He scoffed. "Let's right this wrong now, shall we?" he said, taking hold of my hand.

We found a shop that sold swimwear and Aiden made sure I bought a polka dot bikini set.

"You look..." His roaming eyes made me self-conscious.

"Stop. Don't say anything else."

He laughed loudly. It was plain to see that he was enjoying himself.

"I can't. You look so damn good. I recommend you wear a bikini all the time. Come on," he urged. He ran up to a diving board more than six feet and leapt up into the air before diving neatly into the water. He swam around for some time before re-surfacing. I moved closer to talk to him.

"I don't think I can do that."

"I took lessons with a well-known diver."

"It shows."

"You can try something simpler. A cannonball perhaps. Come on, Simi. You know you want to." He swept back his wet hair to reveal his eyes. He licked his lower lip and winked. That was my signal to get in the water.

"A cannonball then," I said to myself.

"Princess! Catch!"

I was too slow to react, and the incoming ball hit my face. I stepped on something slippery in the process of finding my bearing and the next moment I found myself on the ground.

"Simi!" Aiden was out of the water and by my side. "Are you alright?"

"Yes, yes, I'm fine."

I sounded more annoyed than hurt. When I made to stand up, I felt a sharp stinging pain explode from my ankle.

"I think I sprained my ankle."

Aiden examined my right foot.

"There's a slight swelling," he observed. "You know my blood can..."

"No." I protested as his eyes tried to find mine. "Don't. I'm not that hurt."

He found my eyes at last and did not look convinced.

Chidi's shaky voice startled me. "Princess, I'm so sorry. It was my fault."

"No, it's not. I'm fine. It's just a little bruise."

"Are you sure? What can I do?"

"You can enjoy yourself."

Aiden threw on a shirt and put me in another shirt twice my size.

I winced in pain as he lifted me from the ground.

"What happened?" Amaeka asked.

Aiden explained hastily. "I'm taking her to a hospital. Tell the children they can get anything they want from the mall. I'll see them later."

"Alright."

"Funny thing about children is when you ask them to pick out anything from a store they end up picking candy," he said to me after taking the keys to Amaeka's husband's car.

We got to the nearest hospital in five minutes. The Doctor took a good look at the leg before giving his verdict. I would be in a cast for roughly four weeks and should use crutches if I wanted to get around. Aiden and I waited for the nurse to come and apply the cast.

"Does it hurt badly?"

"Oh yes it does, but the painkillers will help. Thank you for bringing me here but aren't you missing out on your birthday fun?"

"I have to be here with you."

"You didn't have to bring me here. Amaeka or her husband could have easily done that."

He took my left hand in his and squeezed lightly.

"I like being with you. More than I care to admit."

His confession made my heart skip a beat. The nurse came in soon afterwards and set my ankle in a cast.

Back at the orphanage, the children had a field day scribbling their names on it. Chidi's was the boldest with a love sign and his name in it. Aiden brought me down for dinner, which consisted of corned beef macaroni and cake afterwards. We all watched a series about a bunch of children on an island, and within an hour, most of the children were asleep. I was feeling a bit sleepy too, so I asked Aiden to help me back up to my room.

"Thank you," I said as he placed me gently on the bed.

'It's nothing."

"You just brought me up two flights of stairs and didn't break a sweat. Your breathing is more even than mine."

He shrugged it off.

My legs dangled from the bed as I moved further into it. His incredible strength came from being a shape-shifter. I dared not point it out. It did not seem like a topic to pop up at that moment.

"I'm sorry you got hurt."

He got on one knee to observe my ankle. His hands touched the cast, and it looked like he was the one in pain.

"I hate seeing you hurt."

"I'll be fine. I've been through worse haven't I?"

He perked up his head, and I could barely move. His hand was on my calf.

"Thank you Aiden," I said, stroking his hair with the tips of my fingers.

A low sound erupted from him.

He edged closer, gauging my response, his eyes on what he wanted. I closed the distance between us, my fingers still in his hair. Without any more hesitations, his lips were on mine. Warm and soft and soothing. Everything I imagined kissing him would be. He used his free hand to bring me even closer to him and kissed deeper.   When his lips disengaged from mine, I was breathless. For a while, we just stared at each other. I took that as an incentive to go on. This time I initiated the kiss. He played with my tongue and then gently sucked on it. He invaded my senses with that move. Every part of me now yearned for him.

His hands encircled my back, squeezed tight, making every second of the kiss better than the next. I trailed my hand down his neck to his chest, my breath becoming faster.

He stopped, gave me a quick kiss on my cheek and flashed a smile.

"I think I just got the best birthday present ever."

His voice was flooded with heated emotion. I waited before I spoke up knowing well my voice would sound worse.

"Are you sure? Because I saw a pair of boxer briefs, I would love to get you."

His laughter made my heart flutter.

"Goodnight Simi."

"Goodnight," I mumbled.

I spent most of my waking hours trying not to read any meaning to the kiss. It had been a sweet, friendly kiss, and that was it. But deep down I knew there were no such things as soft, affectionate kisses. Not with the way he had kissed me anyway.

The next day we left the orphanage but not after been begged by the children to stay for the rest of the year. A request I was not so eager to decline.

CHAPTER 9

"What in God's name happened to you?" was the first thing Femi blurted out when he saw me get out of my house with a crutch on my right hand. He was wearing white tennis shoes, shorts and a button-down shirt.

"Just a little sprain."

"A little?" His bulging eyes conveyed surprise and anger.

"I'll get better in less than a week so you can rest easy."

"See what happens when you hang around that man? You've suffered many injuries because you were with him."

"Well, not countless."

He furrowed his brows. "How am I supposed to take you to play tennis like this? How? You can't swim properly too, or do anything with that leg."

"You can play table tennis instead, and I'll watch."

"Come here, you stubborn woman. I'll help you into the car."

He no longer looked angry. The fact that I was willing to go with him seemed to quell his mood.

"Thanks."

At the club, we met Mr And Mrs Ajiri, a couple who looked like they were twins. They were the ones who had invited Femi to the club, and they seemed particularly eager to know who I was. Joining them at the alfresco restaurant brought relief to my aching legs. Mrs Ajiri who asked me to call her Philippa inquired about my legs. I told her I fell. "I see you have no ring on your finger. Both of you. How can two good-looking people be unattached?"

Her question made my stomach tighten.

"You have no one in mind, Femi?" she continued asking her uncomfortable questions.

I caught Femi's eyes on me. I tried not to look back at him.

"I have someone in mind. I'll need to be really convincing to get her to say yes."

"I like that," Mr Ajiri added. His lack of interest in the small talk was welcomed by me.

"You should work hard at it. She will not take you seriously if you don't apply yourself," Mrs Ajiri advised.

A man in tight shorts walked up to us and asked Mr Ajiri to play tennis with him, but he politely declined the offer.

"Femi has no one to play with," I shot up immediately, hoping to clear the tension still hanging in the air. "I'm sure he would love to have a match with you."

Femi took up his racket and helped me up from my chair. We said our goodbyes to the Ajiris. I trailed after Femi and his new tennis opponent by the name of Retford. They took positions in the court, and I took my place in the spectator section sitting down on one of the lowest rows of chairs. There was no way I could get up the stairs with my bad leg. Femi waved at me as he twisted his racket this way and that. The game started, and for the next five minutes, my eyes were focused on the two players, but my mind was somewhere else. Was Femi talking about me when Mrs Ajiri asked that question? His demeanour had clearly suggested so. Was I ready for such a commitment? Would I agree to marry Femi if he asked? Do I use my job as a front to push men away?

"Hey."

My heart jumped at the sight of him.

"Oh, Aiden. You have a habit of always showing up," I said.

He was in a hoody and cargo shorts. His tennis shoes gave a new meaning to the word white. I had thought that sharing a passionate kiss with him would bring awkward moments when we met again but seeing him now made me feel more comfortable than embarrassed.

"What are you doing here?"

"I'm here with Femi."

I pointed at Femi, who was going at the game with determination. Aiden did not bother to look. Femi may not have existed for all he cared. He stared down at my aching leg.

"How's the leg?"

"Better."

"You should be resting not out here with some guy."

Was that a hint of jealousy? I smiled.

"Femi is my friend."

He laughed mockingly and said, "Get better."

His eyes became softer, and his furrowed brows disappeared.

I ogled his lips and gulped, swallowing hard. It was almost like I had caught an instant fever, and it was not going away for a very long time. From the corner of my eyes, I saw Femi looking intently at us.

"I have to go," Aiden said, taking my right hand in his and planted a kiss on it.

"Why?" I scolded myself for asking such a ridiculous question. I badly wanted him to stay. His presence never failed to make me feel good from the inside out.

His soft laughter rang in my ears. "I have a meeting to get to. I'll see you."

"Okay," was my faint reply.

I watched as he walked away until he could no longer be seen. My focus returned to the game. Femi was no longer playing with determination but with brute strength. It was frightening to watch.

Every swing of his racket sent Retford cowering with fear. A few minutes later, Retford proclaimed himself the loser and stopped the game.

"You didn't even have to play to win. You sent him running away like a child."

Femi dumped his equipment beside him and stood in front of me fuming. To ask or not to ask was the question that needed serious attention. I knew it could be disastrous and I braced myself for an outburst which I got in full. I asked, "What's wrong?"

"What's wrong? Nothing, Simi. I'm absolutely peachy."

"You're not."

"You're damn right, I'm not. Why him?"

"Why who?"

"You know who I'm talking about."

"I don't know. You tell me," I replied and moved my uninjured leg.

"Aiden Essien. I told you to stay away from him, and now you're in love with him?"

"I'm not," I denied even though part of me knew it was true.

"You cannot be with him. He's dangerous, more than you know."

I suspected something odd, but I eased out of the thought.

"Dangerous? What do you mean?"

He was quiet for a while and tried to keep a calm composure.

"He just is. He's not someone you should be with. His nature cannot be denied."

"What are you talking about Femi?"

His words were starting to clear my doubts. Did Femi know about Aiden's secret and if he did how much did he know? Or maybe it was just ugly jealousy, and I was overreacting.

"It's nothing you should worry about. I'm going to take care of it. I will."

An unknown fear gripped my heart so suddenly, and I felt faint.

"What do you mean? What are you talking about?" I asked, a pain growing in my chest.

"Are you okay?" Femi asked, coming closer.

"Just answer the damn questions, Femi."

He moved a step back and said "I can't. You'll be safe, I promise."

His intense concentration on the steering wheel on the drive back home provided the necessary distraction for him. All I needed to do was look out the window and count the traffic lights.

"Simi," Femi called as I hobbled toward my front door. I refused to look back at him. He started his car and sped away. My anger turned to worry for him.

There were two messages from Ava waiting for me both asking me to call her ASAP. I took up the phone and dialled. Either she was so eager or nervous to spill her guts, her phone fell down. The clattering made me take the phone away from my ear and clicked on 'loudspeaker'.

She talked fast, asking me to invite Aiden for dinner on Sunday at her place to thank him for the 'Orbit gig' and hung up.

There was little time to process the information, and when I did, I realised there was no way I could stay away from Aiden, not even if I wanted to. I called Aiden and was put through to him by Henry.

"So can you make it?"

There was a continuous humming on the background, and there was shouting in a foreign language.

"Can you?"

" .... I mean, yes."

"Thank you." The humming stopped, but the shouting continued incessantly.

"Hey, I gotta go. I'll pick you up on Sunday by six."

"Alright."

Femi came around later that night to apologise. I smelled alcohol on his breath, but who was I to judge? I resulted to the same tactics sometimes under duress.

"You have to go home," I told him sternly.

"I love you, Simi." Femi looked so sad. "I've always loved you. Ever since the first time, we kissed, remember?"

I remembered. It had been a brief kiss between two nervous teenagers who knew nothing about life.

"But you love that rich guy, don't you?" he asked. "Is it because he has more money than me? He does not deserve you, the beast."

Something about that word sounded familiar.

"You should go home, Femi."

His reddened eyes closed halfway and opened up almost immediately.

"Yes, I should go home. No need to bother you with my drunk self." His sheepish smile did a wonder on his appearance. "I love you, Simisola Oladeji."

"Do you want me to drive you home?"

"I'll be fine. I'm not that drunk. Just tired, very tired. Goodnight."

"Goodnight Femi." He waved and staggered back to his car. For someone drunk, he handled the wheels well.
***

Mona came to the door after I rang the doorbell twice. Her eyes opened up as wide as it could possibly allow.

"Oh my god, you're Aiden Essien," she pointed out.

"That I am."

"Good evening to you too Mona."

I ceased to exist from that moment and the next few moments. I was gradually absorbed into the shadow of the man beside me.

"Jessica! Come here!" Mona called.

"What is it? Oh my god, it's Aiden Essien."

Both stood transfixed at the door.

"Can we come in now?" I asked.

"Oh, yes, welcome to our home." Mona took his hand and led him inside.

"Oh, aunt Simi what happened to your leg?" Lisa observed.

"I..."

I noticed her gawking at Aiden, and I gave up.

"Nothing, just go ahead."

"Oladeji's daughter," Jephery greeted.

"Jephery the great," I replied.

"How's the leg?"

"Still useful."

Jephery, who was in the living room, stood up to shake hands with Aiden. The two men started talking, and the girls had to go help their mother set the table. My sister came in, and the first thing she said was "you look better in person than all your pictures."

"Right?" The twins agreed.

"Thank you. Usually, people tell me the opposite," Aiden joked.

"It's what I love about this crazy family of mine," I said to Aiden. "No one is ever discreet. We just say whatever we want to and hope we get away with it."

"Dinner is ready," Ava announced.

"What is this?" Her husband asked.

"Yes, Mrs Eneje. Are we having more guests over?" I asked.

On the table was a buffet—creamy chicken, potatoes, fried rice, prawn pasta and other edibles.

"I just didn't know what Aiden would like so I went all out."

"I'm sure they're all delicious, thank you."

As we ate the twins bombarded Aiden with questions. I found out he had a new excellent quality; tolerance for annoying kids. The crazy thing about it all was that their mother let them ask; all in an attempt to get information too but more subtly.

"Can we come over...to your house?"

"We can arrange that."

"How about tomorrow?" Lisa placed her hands together in a plea. Everyone laughed.

"No," Jephery spoke out at last. "Tomorrow you and your sister are going to the dentist."

"So another time Mister Aiden?" Mona asked.

"Definitely."

After dinner, Ava brought out a banana cake and biscuits to satisfy our sweet tooth. She used that opportunity to thank Aiden for getting her spa into Orbit.

"Don't thank me. I actually did that for my own selfish gain."

"What do you mean?"

"Simi understands." He winked at me.

"Don't listen to him. There was no selfish intent to what he did."

We talked for a while and called it a night.

It was raining gently when he drove me back home and walked me to the door.

"Your sister is an amazing cook."

"I'll say. She has been going at it since she was twelve."

"You don't look so much like her. If I wanted to be blunt, I'd say you don't look like her at all."

"That's true. After my parents got married, they found out it would take a miracle to have any children, so they decided to adopt. Ava came into their lives and then my mum had me a few years after."

"It must have been lovely to have someone like her growing up. She's delightful." "She was pretty bossy and annoying. Now she is delightful."

"Her daughters as well."

"Those two are a scream. Better watch out."

He lingered at the door, and I waited. Waiting for what? I did not know. He leaned forward and stopped when his lips were just inches from mine. My lips parted slightly in anticipation. He lifted his head and placed a kiss on my forehead, right above my eyebrow.

"Goodnight, Simi."

"Sweet dreams, Aiden," I uttered quietly, disappointed.

That kiss was a big step down from the one we had shared, and I had hoped for a repeat performance. Sadly none came.

CHAPTER 10

My mind wandered as I read a new article in the New England Journal of Medicine on the computer. From Aiden to Femi to the awful dreams I had on repeat. Something felt off.

"Simi, what are thinking of?" Nadia asked. Her gossip mode was activated, but she was getting nothing out of me.

"Nothing interesting."

I noticed her burgundy dress and blue ribbon sandals. "Where are you going?"

"I have a date."

"It's almost 11 p.m."

"I know."

"You should be prepping to head home and get some rest."

"No. I need this, Simi. He's just too cute."

"Nadia, can you help me get this typed out? It's urgent."

One of the pharmacists on call handed Nadia a sheet of typing paper.

"Sure," she replied. "I'm still going on my date."

The way she spoke and then pouted made me laugh.

"And I'm going home. The emergency room has become a boring place."

I stared at the two women who sat on the comfy white chairs, reading the fashion magazine strewn out on the brown coffee table. I started picking up my things when my phone rang.

"Aiden."

"When are you getting off work?"

"In about ten minutes."

The nurses replacing us walked through the door.

"I'll pick you up. I have a strange surprise for you. I'll give you a clue. It's made of metal and really dangerous."

"A machine gun?"

"Definitely not."

"I'll meet you at the T-junction."

I hung up and picked up my bag.

There was no one on the road save for the two security guards who were off to work. I walked down the deserted Clinton Street on my way to the junction. The street was known for its vast amount of enormous masquerade trees. The gusting wind made them wave from side to side. The sound of barking dogs made me suddenly aware of my surroundings. I heard a noise and looked up in alarm. There was nothing there except the trees and swaying branches.

I laughed at myself for getting scared.

Headlights coming from behind made me look back. The car sped down my way and stopped in front of me.

The screeching sound made my heart rate triple, and my ears ached. Two men stepped out of the car. The last man waited in the driver's seat. One of the men was bald and had what appeared to be an amulet made of a feather and beads around his neck. The other was younger and much taller.

"Scream, and you die," the young man threatened.

"I have a little money in my bag and my phone," I said, backing away.

There was a lot of laughter from the two men.

"We have come a long way to find you."

"What do you want?"

"She's asking what we want. Just like the rest of them."

The bald man laughed and gave the younger man a knowing look. It was as if I had said something out of ignorance. He mouthed something into the amulet.

"It is really you this time. No doubt about it."

"What is it that you want?"

"Ajë is in you, and you are in her. You possess so much power, and you don't even know it."

I edged backwards in fear, fumbling with the confines of my bag, ready to bring out my newly acquired pepper spray.

"What are you talking about?"

The bald man was done talking.

"Bode." The taller man turned. "Take her."

"Don't come any closer!" I shouted, firing my spray, but instead of the hot peppery liquid squirting out, a bright light emerged from my hands sending the man over the car and all the way to the other lane. The man landed with a ghastly thud.

"What the ..." the words got stuck in my throat. I stared at my hand and threw my pepper spray on the ground. Instinct told me to shout for help, but I was too scared to even move.

The bald man laughed hysterically. The other man behind the wheel came out, circled the car and stood behind the bald man.

"I told you. Raw untapped power. But now you must come with me, Reincarnation of Ajë."

The sound coming from the opposite direction eased my worries. There was a trail of blue light coming from behind it. The motorcycle came to a grinding halt, and Aiden alighted from it. He was wearing a jumper and blue stone-washed jeans, which made him look younger in a boyish way.

"Grab her," the bald man ordered.

I tried to run, but I was held by the driver. His lousy breath made my stomach turn.

"Let her go."

"Go about your own business, Mister Man."

"I said, let her go."

I saw a glint in Aiden's eyes, and it frightened me. His hair gradually turned white. A deep growl came from him.

The pang in my chest was in anticipation of his next move. Would I get to see him transform into his other self?

"Let me go!" I screamed and kicked.

The bald man took a pistol from his jacket and fired at Aiden. The shot was silent, but my high-pitched scream rent the cold night air. My captor covered my mouth with his hand, and I gagged.

Aiden moved swiftly. He was in front of the man with the gun in the blink of an eye and tore it away from his grasp. He gripped the attacker's right arm and snapped it with one swift motion. The bone jutted out of his elbow, and blood spewed out. The man fell to the ground crying and cursing.

"If you want to keep your head," Aiden spoke to the man holding me, "you'll take your friends and leave. You have three seconds."

There was fidgeting behind me. It did not last for long.

"We will come back. The time is almost upon us, and we will get what we want. I assure you, Ajë will be reborn."

He tore away from me and ran to get the bald man into the car and drove to the other lane to get the other one.

My legs gave way beneath me, and I fell to my knees.

"Simi, Simi, are you alright?"

I stared straight through him. My thoughts became chaotic, and I could not remember where I was.

"Simi." Aiden shook me out of my stupor.

"I'm not fine," I told him.

"I can see that. Your foot is better, though."

"Thanks to the painkillers."

He straightened me up.

I ran my hand over his arm where he had been shot. Only a small hole on the sleeve of his jumper told the tale.

"You were shot."

"Just a scratch."

His eyes scrutinised my entire being.

"Do you know those men?"

I shook my head and cleared my throat. There seemed to be something bitter stuck inside trying to get out.

"What were they talking about?"

"I don't know."

The dream I had the day I first met Aiden, and the aftermath of it came streaming back.

"We should go," Aiden said.

"Your surprise?" I asked as I climbed atop the motorcycle.

"Yes, I was hoping to show it to you under different circumstances."

My mind went back to the bright light that had emerged from my hand and what it did. Aiden took my hands, and I trembled. He wrapped them around his body, bringing me back from my disturbing thoughts. I smiled and laid my head on his back.

Femi was waiting for me on my front steps when we pulled in front of my house. His countenance changed when he saw Aiden holding me and helping me walk.

"What did you do to her?" Femi charged forward, enraged.

I stepped in between them and frowned.

"He did nothing. What are you doing here by this time anyway?"

His voice came down to a whisper.

"I came to apologise for what happened the other day."

"You're forgiven," I told him hastily.

"I'm not leaving you with him," he said, looking Aiden's way.

I could hear the growling clearly now.

"Just stop it the both of you. Your negative energy is making me sick."

"What happened to you?"

"Can we talk inside? My leg hurts."

Once inside, Aiden went about the kitchen like he knew every corner of it. He filled the kettle with water and turned on the gas. I was sitting on a high stool with Femi who was not trying to hide his distaste for Aiden.

"Now tell me all that happened."

I told Femi everything, omitting the supernatural part.

"I think they were just small-time thieves trying to get some money. Thanks to Aiden, they left me alone."

Aiden placed his hands on the kitchen top and said "One of the men mentioned something about an Ajë. The supposed small-time thieves said they will be back for her."

Well, the cat was out of the bag.

"Did you just say Ajë?" Femi shot up from his stool.

"Yes, maybe I'm not pronouncing it correctly. He said something about Ajë being reborn. Those guys looked like they were going to use Simi for some voodoo magic ritual. Do you know anything about it?"

Femi paced from one end of the kitchen to the other. The shrill sound of the boiling water became apparent, and Aiden turned off the gas. He searched the cupboards and found a box of tea and proceeded to get it ready.

"Femi what do you know about this Ajë?"

"I don't..." He was clearly hiding something.

I groaned in frustration. "Something impossible happened out there tonight, and I need answers. Please, Femi."

Aiden handed me a steaming cup of tea. I flashed him a weak smile as thanks. I blew on it and drank. He had added a copious amount of honey in it, just the way I liked it.

"I'll tell you all that I know," Femi started with a sigh. "This information has been passed down from my ancestors down to their descendants. Long ago, there was a mighty witch. She could turn into anything she wanted and enter people's homes to drink their blood."

"You mean like a vampire?"

"Sort of. The victims became sick and died in days. The blood was the source of her powers. It made her more powerful but on a small scale. She discovered a clan where she could get insurmountable powers. Their blood made her stronger than she ever was, and she hooked on it, like a drug." He paused to regain his breath. "This clan knew that they would soon die out if they did nothing about it. There was no way to kill the witch, so they used their magic to seal her away."

"So she's indestructible?"

"Yes. There's only one weapon that can kill her, but one would be unwise to go on such a journey to get it. Very unwise, indeed."

"She's still alive?" Aiden inquired. He blinked his tired eyes and rubbed his temple in smooth motions.

"Technically."

"What does it have to do with me?"

I drank my warm tea and coughed.

He explained. "The witch's name was Ajë. It was predicted by a seer among my people that she would come back, but no one knew how or when."

I threw the last dregs of the tea down my throat and passed the cup to Aiden whose eyes had been fixed on me the whole time.

"The men told me that I was her and she was me. What does that mean?"

"It means you, Simi Oladeji, are a witch and a pretty powerful one at that. She must have sealed her powers or part of her consciousness into you.

From the knowledge passed down to me by my grandfather, the only way to completely do such a thing is with a pregnant woman. That would mean one of your ancestors was prey to the witch."

"The clan you mentioned, they had a name, did they not?"

Femi turned to Aiden and said "the clan was called Meje. Beasts the whole lot of them were. Bloodthirsty, filthy beasts."

"Aiden." My voice was shrill.

Aiden's calm demeanour almost fooled me. I knew he was distraught.

"Were they all slaughtered?" I probed some more.

"Yes."

"By who?"

"By my ancestors."

My body went stiff. "Why would they do that?"

"Because the Meje people were the scum of the earth and had to be eradicated. My ancestors were all servants of the earth goddess, Yemaja. Well, they didn't do a good job of it because the last of their kind is here in this room with us."

"I thought you were a devout Catholic."

"Well, some things just have to be done for the greater good," he answered calmly.

"How do you know I am one of them?" Aiden's voice was unrecognisable.

He was too choked up to bring his voice to normal.

"Because this—" he lifted his vest and let his birthmark come into view, "—grows an inch longer every time you turn into that filth. And with every inch, the pain gets worse. Even standing close to you makes it burn. The mantle of Chief Hunter fell upon me, and I had to perform my duty, but I could not. I do not possess the will my ancestors had. I do not believe in killing innocent people." He glanced at Aiden. "If my grandfather were as strong as he used to be, he would have killed you the moment he saw you and end all this."

"What do you mean?"

My pulse quickened, and sweat broke out on my forehead even though the room was cold.

"Don't you understand?" was Femi's answering question. "You with him, it's all perfect for them. It's like serving them what they want on a diamond platter. His ancestors put Ajë away, and they'll need his blood to bring her back." He laughed in a nerve-jangling manner. "For Ajë to come back they'll need you and him."

It all dawned on me that meeting Aiden may have been no coincidence, neither was meeting Femi. Everything was being pieced together for one single purpose.

Femi's said with a straight face, "I could end it all by killing him."

"I'd like to see you try," retorted Aiden, his harsh voice slicing through my ears.

"Or you could kill me," I retorted standing up.

Femi turned to face me and said, "I can't kill you."

"Well since you're so bent on killing someone you can add me to the list too."

"Don't say that."

"Then don't you dare lay a finger on him." I choked up.

"This is serious, Simi. This is reality, and bad things happen in reality."

"On the contrary, I do know it. And I know Aiden, and he's not a monster."

"You know what he is and you still stay with him? He must have you hypnotised or something."

"I'm not hypnotised. Don't be absurd."

"He may hurt you."

"I will never hurt her." Aiden's pronouncement made my heart leap.

"Oh." Femi's gaze shifted from me to Aiden and back to me.

"This is what we are going to do?" I began. "Aiden, you'll take me to your library. I need to know everything I can about this. Including your notes taken during your research. And Femi, you'll come too."

"I don't..." Femi tried to back out.

"You'll come too, Femi. I need you to fill in the blanks please."

"Fine."

"I'll take some days off work. I don't think I'll be able to concentrate with this on my mind."

"I'll make the call for you," Aiden offered.

"Thanks."

I went into my bedroom and packed a duffel bag with only the essentials; clothes, toothbrush, some makeup. My hands froze when I reached for the extra charger for my phone. I quickly shook it off and grabbed the cord. This was no time to be freezing up.

I went back to the kitchen to find Aiden and Femi whispering. They both turned my way when I walked in.

There we were in my kitchen, the messed up trio in an even messier love triangle; the Hunter, the witch incarnate and the shape-shifter. And on my heels were bat shit crazy men ready to do anything to bring back an old witch. Fun times.

"I need to take care of a few things first before I fill in your blanks," Femi said.

"Thank you," I replied.

"Everything is going to be alright," he added.

"I want to believe that. Let's go," I said to Aiden.

We got out of the house, and I locked the doors. I got on the motorcycle with Aiden and took a last glance at Femi. He gave a reassuring nod before Aiden drove off.

CHAPTER 11

I did not know how long I had slept, but when I opened my eyes, Aiden's eyes were on me. I shifted in the comfy chair, and the book I had been reading fell to the floor.

"You've made it a habit of yours to be the first person I see anytime I wake up after a tragedy."

"Does it bother you?"

"No, it's comforting."

I noticed the bags under his worn eyes and asked, "Have you had any sleep?"

"I don't need it."

"You look really tired. You don't have to watch over me like a hawk."

"We're the only ones here, so I think I do."

"I don't think I'm ever going to leave this library."

"It's almost 10am. You should have some breakfast. I'll cook."

"I'm not hungry."

"A shower then."

I sniffed.

"I think so. Did you know that there was a time in Nigerian history when women who were believed to be witches were hunted down and decapitated? Just like the witch trials,"

"Yes."

"It's bizarre to think in a different time I would have been hunted down and killed. Oh, wait. It's no different than what I'm going through right now,"

I picked up the book from the floor. On the cover were distorted images. Inside was information enough to warp my brain. The author talked about witches and their innate strength, but nothing about the transfer of powers.

"I saw it," He said,

"What did you see?"

"I saw the light come out of your hands and what it did to that low life."

Stretching out my legs brought comfort to my aching body. I stifled a yawn and looked past him to the door behind. "I don't think I want to talk about it."

"I know you're scared, but I will protect you, Simi. Against anything. Even myself."

"I know that. I just need to learn more about what is inside me."

I stood up from the chair and looked around. Aiden sat on the chair and pointed me in the right direction.

"You can find books about witches and shape-shifters up there."

I climbed the step ladder and looked through the top shelves. I found a book I thought got what I needed."

"You really should get some sleep," I told him as I came down the ladder.

I need not have said that because Aiden was already asleep, his head slightly bent over his shoulder and a peaceful look I envied on his face.

"Sweet dreams," I whispered quietly.

***

Femi arrived at Aiden's house just after noon. By then, Aiden was awake. I had taken a quick shower and was hungry. But hunger tended to fade in the face of death. I joined them in the study on the first floor. Femi stood near the shelves like he was ready to leave at a moment's notice. His eyes kept darting toward the door.

"Do you want a drink?" Aiden offered.

"No, thanks," Femi refused. He faced me. "What have you learnt so far?"

I told him all that I had learned. From Aiden's books to Google searches.

"I know you can make someone a witch through food. Or an item they would not easily notice. I never saw anything like what you told me. A transfer of power that lingers through the generations?"

"That's because she is different. Ajë is powerful. These other witches are nothing compared to her. We're talking about a witch that used blood magic for two centuries."

"Blood magic, is that bad?"

"The worst. Blood magic tends to be shunned by witches. It allows you to manipulate things without going through the proper channels. It eats away at your very soul and disturbs the fabric of nature itself."

"Can I transfer it? Maybe into another witch or a vessel?"

Femi laughed.

"What kind of vessel?"

"I read that you can transfer consciousness into a doll."

"Yes. When it's yours. This consciousness. This power within you is another's."

"And a witch?"

"No witch will willingly take the power of a blood witch. It's like taking on an infection."

"That's a nice mental picture," Aiden said.

"Even if you wanted to forcefully do it, you'd have to find a witch first. And they aren't exactly the welcoming type."

"I think I saw her once," I said in a low voice. "The first time I met Aiden. That fire was no fabric static. The encounter nearly burnt my house down."

"And if she does come back and gets her hand on you, worse things will happen."

"Then I have to use her powers against her."

"What do you mean?" Aiden asked, leaning against mahogany the table.

"I've been thinking about it ever since Femi told me who Ajë is. Now I know I cannot just give her powers and consciousness away. I can clearly use it. I don't know how I did what I did, but I can try to use it."

"You shouldn't be using her powers," Femi cautioned. "It will corrupt you."

I clenched my teeth in frustration.

"What other choice do we have?"

"We can protect you."

"Oh, please," I scoffed. "I've got this tremendous energy flowing through me, and I'll be a fool if I don't use it to protect myself. I don't want what happened to me yesterday to ever happen again. Those men deserve to have a taste of their own medicine."

"It's dangerous."

"Don't you think I know that? You have to help me. You obviously know more than you are letting on."

Femi crossed his arms.

"She won't give up," Aiden told him.

"Don't you think I know that?"

He sighed and uncrossed his arms. "Maybe there is something I can do. I've seen my grandmother do it all the time. It's mostly up to you, but I'll need certain items."

"What exactly are we going to do?"

"We'll carry out a small ritual. To draw out some of your powers. Not everything."

"When?" I asked eagerly.

"This evening."

"Why not now?"

My stomach answered for me.

"I'll bring what is needed this evening. Eat something."

Femi did not wait to be shown out. He hurried out of the house as if something was after him.

"I'll make some food," Aiden said and headed for the kitchen.

I went down to the library and took a book on witchcraft. I returned to the kitchen and sat at the island reading and watching Aiden slice and dice.

"What you want Femi to do is dangerous."

I put the book down next to the vase of flowers.

"More dangerous than those men after me?"

"I don't know."

"I have to do this."

I picked the book back up and began reading about the witch culture in Yoruba land.

Ten minutes later, I had a plate of scrambled eggs, toasted bread and orange juice in my front. I wolfed down the food in no time and got back to reading.

By 6pm, Femi was back. He brought with him some items in a small black bag.

"We have to do this in an open space," he told Aiden,

We all went down to the grassy field next to the tennis court. Femi looked up at the sky.

"Here," he said, choosing a portion of the field.

He brought out three red candles which he lit with a gas lighter and placed them strategically on the ground,

"Stand in the middle," he ordered.

I did, and the flickering flames from the candles shot up like birthday sparkles.

Femi handed me something covered in what I believed to be feathers.

"Is this safe?" Aiden asked.

Femi ignored him.

"Don't look at it. Squeeze tight and call forth your power."

"How?" I asked.

"Call it Simi. Use your mind."

"Call it," I muttered. "Call it." How do I call it?

"You might want to stand back," Femi told Aiden.

I squeezed the small object, and in my mind, I called the power within me. I kept remembering what I did to the man who attacked me. The way he got knocked out. That awful sound that followed. The object in my hand shrunk with every passing second. When it finally disappeared, I closed my eyes, and when I opened them, the green grass around me had turned black.

"It is done," Femi said.

I smiled and took a step forward but came crashing down. Aiden and Femi rushed to help me up.

"I'm fine," I told them standing up on my own. I felt more energised than I had ever been before. "So, what now?" I asked.

"Now, you learn to use your powers."

I stretched out my hand like I did before, but nothing happened.

"It may take a while."

"Thank you Femi," I said and hugged him.

"Thank you," Aiden said and offered a hand. Femi looked at Aiden's limb for a second then shook it.

I smiled and said, "I should lie down."

I took a few steps toward the house then noticed no one was following me. I turned around to see Aiden and Femi rooted to where they stood, their mouths gone.

"Dear God!" I gasped holding my stomach.

Femi tried to say something with his eyes.

"What?"

He moved his eyes downward.

"Oh."

I straightened up and hurried to touch both of them, willing them to move and talk again. They both gasped at the same time,

"I'm so sorry. I did not know when I did that."

They stared at me in a way that brought chills to my body.

"It's going to be alright," Aiden assured me.

"You'll have to master your abilities," Femi added. "I did not enjoy having my mouth disappear."

Femi picked up the candles and placed them in the bag.

"I'll be back tomorrow. Don't kill anyone. Except for him. I don't mind if you kill him."

Aiden laughed. "Good one," he said.

We watched Femi leave.

Aiden turned to me and tried to hug me, but I moved away from his reach.

He put his hands on his hips and chuckled.

"I'll be inside," I told him.

"I want to hold you," he said coming after me.

"No, Aiden no."

At first, I told him off in a severe tone, but he was bent on making the mood light. He grinned and kept on walking faster.

"No," I laughed and walked ahead.

He ran faster and tackled me from behind. He lifted me off from the ground and swung me around.

"Godammit Aiden!"

I squealed and pushed myself away from him. He let me go. I stared at him, looking for any damages.

He opened his arms and dropped them.

"I'm fine, Simi. Come on. I'll open a bottle of wine and heat up the food in the fridge."

"You're sure you're fine?"

"I am," he replied.

We walked side by side into the house.

I helped Aiden put the food in the microwave while he brought a bottle of white wine from the cellar. We sat down in the kitchen drinking wine until the microwave dinged.

I set up the plates and drinking glasses on the kitchen island and dished out the rice and chicken.

"Thank you," Aiden said and began eating. I sat opposite him and chewed slowly. When I reached out for my glass, it shattered. I stood up immediately.

"Are you hurt?" he asked.

"No."

"I'll clean it up."

"No, I'll do it myself. You don't happen to have plastic cups do you?"

He shook his head.

"I'll probably melt them," I grumbled to myself.

I cleared up the mess and ate quickly. Then I headed to my room and locked the door behind me. I took a deep breath, feeling the surge of energy from the tips of my fingers to that of my toes.

I focused my attention on the curtains. Fire. All I thought about was fire. The bottom of the curtains started to burn. I gasped and laughed at the same time.

Maybe I could master my abilities faster than I thought.

I poured water over the curtains. I remembered they were not mine and tried to figure out the expense for fixing them.

I shook my head and decided to have a long bath.

The slight tapping on my door as I exited the bathroom made me shudder. I towel-dried my hair and threw on a bathrobe before opening the door.

"Tea?" Aiden began offering me a cup of tea. It smelled lemony.

"Thanks."

I left the door open so he could come in.

"Wanna talk about it?" he asked

"Talk about what?"

He joined me on the chaise lounge sofa by the window. I sipped my tea, eyes on his moving lips.

"Your trembling hands, shattering glasses, making mouths disappear. This cannot be easy for you."

No, it was not.

"It's for the greater good," I answered. "Those men will definitely come back, and I need something in my arsenal."

"You're angry."

"Yes, I'm angry. And scared. But I will not go down without a fight."

"Me neither."

"For now, we can just stay here, drink some tea and talk about anything else."

"That sounds nice."

"Or you can kiss me."

He dropped his cup of tea and faced me squarely.

"I was hoping to kiss you again."

"Not another forehead kiss, I hope."

"Looking the way you do now? No. Just don't take my mouth away."

I rolled my eyes. But I hoped I would not lose control and do just that.

His unblinking eyes were hypnotic. He reached for my hair and traced his fingers down my face.

"Aiden," I moaned, spilling some tea on the robe. I stood up in haste, setting aside the teacup on the dressing table. The gown had quite a significant stain on it.

Aiden walked up to me, not minding that I was fussing with the robe and lamenting my clumsiness.

He cupped my face in his hands and planted his lips on mine without saying a word. They were searing hot.

Hot and soft and oh so delicious. A deep moan escaped my lips as he ran his tongue in my mouth, exploring and tasting. And then another as he deftly pulled the robe apart.

His warm hands on my body sent shock shaves down to the tips of my toes. I could not get enough of whatever he was doing down there with his fingers that drove me senseless. I understood what desire meant. Such a simple word, yet it carried such intense meaning. I did not know how we got to bed, but I realised how wet I had become.

His feather-like kisses behind my ears moved down to my navel, making me writhe from the mind-numbing pleasure. He was down there again, doing something incredible with his tongue. My legs on their own accord spread open. His fingers massaged my thighs as I dug mine into his bulging biceps. His tongue slid from between my legs and up to my belly button. And then in between my breasts.

His hardness brushed against my thighs. He drew me closer to him and seeing the desire for me in his eyes took away the ability to see anything but him.

"Aiden," I called his name again and again until it merged with my breathing.

He intertwined his fingers with mine and smiled. He knew how badly I desired him, but he wanted to drive me to the edge. He released me from his grip so I could take off his clothes. My hands trembled so much he ended up doing it himself.

"Simi." He kissed me, his hands around my neck, his warmth burning through my skin.

I licked my lips, completely hypnotised by what I saw before me.

His held my gaze as his fingers trailed down my chest stopped underneath my breasts. He cupped them without breaking focus, and I gasped. I lost all control.

I wanted every part of him as soon as he was willing to give it to me.

He scooped me up into his arms so that my legs wound around him as he knelt on the bed.

The incredible sensation that accompanied his firm yet gentle thrusts propelled my body into a seismic convulsion. So much wetter now. I could feel his hands entangle my hair as I clasped my legs and tightened my arms around his body. My sanity was gone, and so was his.

CHAPTER 12

Aiden was still atop me when he slowly opened his beautiful glazed eyes. His breathing was uneven as he spoke.

"You are the most incredible person to ever walk into my life."

He kissed me and fell to his side. I moved over and rested my head on his chest. He wound his right arm around me and pulled me in. I shivered when his body touched mine.

"Why did you become a nurse?"

He gently played with my hair.

"Why are you asking?" I chuckled.

"I want to know. I want to know everything about you." He sounded sleepy.

"I get to help people, save lives. It does not get better than that, at least for me, it doesn't. The job does have its rainy days though, but we get through it."

"Hmmm," Aiden hummed.

"I'm thinking of going back to school, become a doctor."

"You know I'll always be here for you, supporting you. Whatever career path you choose." He pulled me closer.

"Even if I decide to go to clown school? Entertain children at parties?"

"Especially then. I like clowns."

"What about you?"

"Me?"

"Wanna change your career?"

"It'd be impossible. I pretty much did not have a choice in my career path, but I am proud of where I am today." He paused, kissing my forehead. "I'm so glad you're here."

I liked his honesty and told him that.

"There's no reason to keep what I feel to myself, it's bad for the skin," he added jokingly.

His body shuddered as he laughed, and in a few seconds, I could hear light snoring.

***

I was myself, but strangely, I was not. I could feel my body, but it was not mine, and yet it felt oddly like mine. I was walking down a narrow path with the dew on the tall grasses brushing against my bare arms and feet. With every step I took, I heard a rattling noise, like bells had been tied to my feet. The path gave way before me to reveal a diverging path whose entrance was made of palm fronds carefully crafted together. I went under it with no fear of what awaited me on the other side even though it appeared dark because of the clusters of trees.

The sudden appearance of a scrawny old man in my path should have but did not scare me. The man spoke a distinct sort of Yoruba, yet I understood him. I replied to his greeting, absent-minded.

"No sacrifice has been brought to me, and I have come to ask why you are playing with your life?"

"Ajë, we have sent enough of our children to die at your hands. We will not send more. You may have succeeded in crossing the first barrier, but you cannot cross the next."

The man's eyes flickered, and he clenched his jaw tightly. A burning rage filled my body, and it came out in a sporadic chant that sent the old man reeling in pain. I wanted to stop, but I had no control over my body.

"Stop! Stop it you're killing him!" I shouted, but it all came out silently. She had taken my voice.

My eyes flew open, but my body was no longer on the bed. I looked down to find I was nearly four feet above the ground and floating gently, almost weightless. I panicked and fell to the mattress with a thud.

Aiden was on the floor, a blanket covering his body, and he was coughing hard. His hands were on his throat, and he was reeling in pain just like the old man had done, and I realised what I was doing; choking the life out of him without even touching him. My mouth became drier as I screamed his name. Years of studying in nursing school had taught me how to attend to someone choking but never prepared me on what to do when I caused the choking through magic.

I knelt close to him, my heart racing. My hands trembled, but what made me more afraid was the inner joy I felt from seeing him that way. It was as if I had become one with the witch, and all her emotions were being channelled through me. His eyes turned a brighter shade of yellow. His hair was gradually turning silver with every painful breath he tried to take.

"Aiden," I wept and brought myself to touch him. He instantly stopped choking, scurrying away from my touch.

"I'm so sorry," I sobbed. "I did not mean to do that."

The colour that was lost from his face returned, and he almost looked like himself again. He stretched his hand, and I backed away from him, standing up to my feet.

"I might hurt you again."

He stood up and pulled me into his embrace.

"You can never hurt me, Simi."

"But I just did," I sobbed. "I just did."

"Shhhh..." He hushed me up and kissed my forehead.

"I need to get out of here. Be as far away from you as possible."

He put on his trousers and wrapped me with the blanket. His hands guided me up the stairs. He placed me gently on the sofa and moved toward the door to press a button. The drawn curtains slid open to reveal the infinity pool.

"Simi, you're shaking." His calm, sweet voice unsettled me.

"For someone who almost died, you're really taking it well."

"How else am I supposed to take it?"

"I don't know! Get angry, I guess. Do something but look at me that way."

I buried my face in my palms and sniffed.

He lifted my face with both hands.

"I can't do that. Whatever is happening to you is just something we have to get through. I won't let you feel bad about this."

"You should stay away from me. It'll be the most logical thing to do. I'll understand."

He laughed and hugged me tightly.

"Throwing my own words back at me, are you? That'll be most foolish of me."

I breathed in his musky scent, and I felt calmer.

"I've never felt so vulnerable in my life. Yet from this vulnerability, this weakness comes a strong desire to protect you. I cannot... I will not lose you."

He pulled me down with him, so we both lay on the couch, his arms around me. I clung desperately to him as if the next moment, he would disappear and ended up sleeping like a baby.

The sun slowly rising to herald the morning woke me up. Aiden stirred behind me. I tiptoed from him, and for a whole minute, I stared at his face, which was gently caressed by the warm ray of the sunlight. He looked so beautiful with his hair thrown across his forehead. I could not believe he was on the verge of dying a few hours ago. A smile crept up his mouth, and he licked his lips, an action that made me think of the things he had done with it the previous night.

"Isn't it rude to stare?" There was a cheerful note in his voice.

"Didn't think you were awake."

He lifted his eyelids, and his smile widened.

"I'll have to take a shower. Get you off me."

His laughter rang softly as I took to the stairs.

"I should join you," he offered.

"That is a recipe for more sex."

"You do know you'll just end up back there in a few hours, right?"

He was not letting go, and he was right. Last night had opened up a gateway into something more beautiful than what I had imagined. My life was heading for a turnaround, part of which I liked and the other part I wished would just go away.

The sound of a sonorous breath-taking song drew me to the living quarters after I dressed up. Aiden had changed too and was now staring into the distance.

I enjoyed the view for as long as I could. When he turned around, he flashed white teeth and said, "Agnes Obel, you like?"

"Yes. It's very profound."

He asked me to dance with him. I gladly obliged and for a while shuffled my feet around until he dropped a bombshell.

"I love you, Simi," he confessed. "So much that I don't even know what to do with myself. I am madly in love with you."

I froze. My hand in the air dropped back down slowly back to my side. I was at a loss for words. 'Say those words back' my mind kept screaming at me, but I remained silent, utterly dumbfounded.

Aiden was in love with me. I stood there, unmoving and unblinking.

He waited. His eyes were on me. Heart racing joyfully, a smile, and then an awful wave of panic.

"You don't have to say it back."

"Aiden, I..."

"Come on, let's dance." I moved along with him. He sniffed my hair and said, "you are so beautiful, Simisola Oladeji."

I summoned the courage to look up at him. I pushed myself up to my toes and planted a kiss on his lips. It nagged me at the back of my mind why I refused to tell Aiden that I loved him. The reason was right there in our faces, taunting us. I just could not bring myself to admit my love for Aiden for fear of the permanence that it brought. Maybe I was just crazy.

***

Femi knew.

Or I thought he did. The way he kept glancing at Aiden and me was enough to stir suspicions. Or maybe he stared because of the way Aiden stood beside me.

"She shattered a glass cup and set fire to the curtains," Aiden recounted the horror show. "Then she tried to kill me. Levitated and everything."

"You levitated?"

I told him about my dream.

"I told you this would happen. This power is not yours. It will corrupt you, and soon you will have no control over it."

"I'm doing a good job of controlling it now," I retorted.

"I can see that," he mocked.

"Fighting will get us nowhere," Aiden jumped in. "Simi has to get back to work in two days. I told her it would be safer for her to come and work for me, but she said she'd rather die. Her exact words."

"I'll keep my job, thank you. This," I pointed at the Aiden and myself, "does not spill into our careers."

There was that look again from Femi.

He spoke up. "If there are no incidents in the next 48 hours, then you can freely rejoin the world."

"Good," I said with my head held high.

Two days came and went without another incident. It took a lot of willpower, but I did it. Only then was I cleared by Femi to go back to work.

CHAPTER 13

"What in the world is wrong with you?"

I squinted and groaned painfully in response to Nadia's words.

"So, let me get this straight. You spent your sabbatical at Aiden's mansion. Supposedly had the time of your life…"

I might have omitted an incident or two about my time with Aiden.

"Then he told you he loved you and you didn't say it back because of what exactly?"

Her judgmental look was the best. Nadia picked up another meat pie from her plate and chewed meticulously. We were having lunch together at a restaurant, a short distance from St. Cloud.

"You love him, don't you? Because I know I do."

"Being with him is like being on a special kind of high. It's beyond overwhelming the effect he has on me."

"Then why all the hesitation?"

"I don't know. I guess I was scared to admit it."

"Scared? Of what? Love?"

"Yes, maybe."

I wasn't scared of love, just of what was happening to me and how it affected him. I loved him and despised him at the same time, and I could not help but feel both ways. I had no control over my feelings of loathing because they were not mine in the first place. It was one of the reasons why I was not ready to jump on the love wagon just yet.

"That's insane. He's a good man, I know it. It doesn't even make any sense," she said, her expression completely grim.

"I've had a bad rapport with the male folk since time immemorial. Something keeps popping up to end it all. Most of my relationships just tend to commit suicide. "

Nadia absorbed what I was saying and asked, "Then why drive Aiden away? He seems like a perfectly good guy."

"He is. He's perfect."

I needed to explain to Nadia my complicated feelings and ended up telling her a fraction of the truth. "It's just that when he told me he loved me, I just thought it was too good to be true. It'll just end like the others. Brief and with a broken heart."

"I don't think so. I've never heard any bad report of him with women, and I have double checked. I mean there's little news about him because he tends to keep his private life out of the media, but there's no scandal. Any relationship he's had is non-existent, so he being so open about his feelings for you tells a special kind of story."

There was a brief moment of silence.

"I've never told you this Oladeji, but I loved someone once."

"Are you even capable of that emotion?" I giggled.

"Yes, once a long time ago. He was a nice enough guy, and I loved him, but I wanted other things; soul enriching things."

"You mean money."

"Yes. After being exposed to this world, I got to know that money makes iron float."

"Do you miss him?"

"Sometimes, but I have my expensive shoes and clothes to keep me company. You definitely have to tell Aiden how you feel." She paused for a moment and asked, "How was the sex?"

"Nadia!"

"What? You knew I was going to ask."

I knew that.

"It was, out of this world."

There was a series of giggling from her which stopped abruptly.

"Guess who just walked in here?"

"Who?"

. "Danny."

He saw us and waved. Ever since Danny brought his cousin to the hospital, he kept on showing up at the hospital at odd times even though his cousin had been discharged. He was what you'd call a pervert with a heart of gold. He usually says the first naughty thing that pops up into his mind but other than that he was alright.

"I didn't see you girls in there, so I asked and was directed here."

"Danny, what are you doing here?"

"As usual I wanted to say hi to both of you. I was just passing through."

"Liar," Nadia hissed. "You better leave. I'm about to resume my shift.'

"Your lips are moving, but your seductive eyes are doing all the talking."

"I don't have time for this. My shift has ended. I'm leaving," I told Nadia.

Danny's eyebrows flew up.

"Why? I was going to invite you both to my house for a sandwich; you, me and her in the middle."

"Just be glad it's us you said that to," I said and stood up, "and not other women who would chew you up and spit you out like spoiled food. One of these days you're gonna be hit with a lawsuit Danny. When that happens, I think you'll learn to filter your words. Nadia, I'm off."

"I'll call you. Tell him."

"Tell who what?" I heard Danny ask Nadia as I walked out into the afternoon. The clouds gave signs of an impending downpour, and people hurried about their businesses trying not to get caught in the storm. I had noticed the two men behind me as I ran to get to the tram station on time. They were in long-sleeved shirts and plain trousers hoping to appear inconspicuous, but I knew who they were; bodyguards sent by Femi. As if the ones hired by Aiden were not enough, I was resigned to my fate, not wanting to stir up any trouble.

While in the tramcar, Nadia's voice kept echoing in my head 'Tell him.'

"Adams Avenue," I told the driver of the cab changing my direction from home to Aiden.

Henry answered the door and scrutinised me thoroughly with his dull calculating eyes before letting me in.

"He's upstairs."

"Aren't you going to announce my presence?"

"We both know that's not needed," he said, taking to his right and leaving me with my own blurry thoughts.

I took calm decisive steps up to Aiden's room and pushed the door open. He had a towel wrapped around his waist. His tie, shirt and suit were placed across the bed. His bare body glistened from all the wet.

"Hey," I said, taking a stepping over the threshold.

His smile lit up his clean-shaven face. It was his weapon of destruction to my sanity.

"I was just thinking of you, and here you are."

"Are you on your way out?"

"Yes," he replied, planting a kiss on my neck.

"Then it can wait."

"I would miss a thousand meetings for you. What is it?" his eyes probed. "Come sit."

He took his clothes from the bed and placed them on a chair. We eased to the edge of the mattress.

"It's nothing serious. I ... I just wanted to thank you, for everything you've done for me; for saving my life more than once. For being you. And also for seeing me as someone worthy of your love."

That was not what I wanted to say. I had sounded like a machine. It felt rehearsed. But Aiden gave me a charming smile and held my hand in his.

"I have a feeling that was not what you wanted to say."

"No, not really."

"It's alright if you don't want to tell me now, but I'll let you know this. For a long time, I was alone, and that ceased to be so when you came into my life. You are the centre of my world Simi, and I have no other choice than to orbit around you."

There it was again, a declaration of his affection and I came up with squat.

He tilted my face up to him and kissed me. My fingers knotted into his hair, pulling him closer. He gave a deep-throated groan and bit my lower lip.

"You will be late," I whispered.

"I think I can spare some time," he said with a low moan.

Thirty minutes later, Aiden was out of the door to my disappointment. He had asked me to stay the night, so I could have dinner with him, and I said yes.

I was accosted by Henry on my way to the infinity pool. There was something eerie about him. Maybe he could never smile.

"I'm here just for tonight."

I did not know why I was so eager to tell him the truth.

"I know. Master Aiden already told me."

"Oh, alright, then."

"He loves you. I doubt you can fully comprehend the meaning of those words."

I doubted it too.

"Master Aiden is very different. I have a strong feeling you understand what I mean by that word."

"Yes, he told me everything."

"He may have chopped off a bit or two of the unpleasant part. It's not easy for him being what he is. And telling you his most precious secret must mean that he trusts you. Can I trust you, Miss Simi?"

It felt like I was having a conversation with Aiden's father.

"Yes. Yes, you can."

He opened up. "His transformations leave him tired and weak for a long time, and as he gets older, it gets worse. One time he tried to control his hunger. He tried with all the strength he could muster to keep the monster at bay. But when he knew he could no longer do it because he was losing his senses. I mean literally seeing things. He had to let go, and I got him under chains just in time to stop him from ripping my throat out."

There was a sudden pain in my chest as I pictured Aiden going through a torturous event like that occasionally.

"All night he howled and growled and tried to break free, and when morning came, he had broken most of his ribs."

"Why are you telling me all this?"

"Because I want you to know what you're getting yourself into, not to scare you away but to caution you.

If you know all this and still want to be with him then I can work with that."

"I want to," I told him without thinking.

He responded with something similar to a nod.

"If you need me, I'll be in the kitchen. Have a wonderful evening, Miss Simi."

I found a bubble chair by the pool and slumped into it. Aiden had deliberately left out details of his other side, but I could understand why. It was heartbreaking to think about all he'd been through ever since he came to know his otherworldliness existed. I could not begin to imagine the pain.

I was out there on the terrace, watching the sun slowly sink into the western horizon. The dark clouds were gone. The orange and red hue smeared across the sky looked like the work of a child playing with paint.

"I came a long way hoping to find my son here, but it seems I came at the wrong time. Typical."

Turning the chair around, I met the gaze of the most beautiful woman I had ever seen. She was in a brown sheath dress that hugged her body and revealed her long straight legs. Around her neck was a pink shawl wrapped elegantly to fall on her shoulders. She really was Aiden's mother no doubt. To me, she looked more like Aiden's sister than his mother. Her blond curly hair hung away from her oval face. The only thing that showed her advancement in age was the wrinkles around her eyes when she forced a fake smile.

What kind of genes did this family possess?

The wind lifted part of the shawl up, and I saw the scar on her neck. I pitied her. To be reminded every day of what her son almost did to her. Of what her son was.

She clutched her heart-shaped purse in a manner that propagated the presence of royalty.

"Hello," I said, not knowing what else to say.

"Hi there." Her smirk rattled me. "You must be the pretty little thing my son has taken a fancy to."

"I'm Simisola Oladeji, ma'am."

"You are prettier than she described."

'She' I knew was Emmeline Zimmerman.

"Thank you."

"That was not a compliment young lady. I'll get straight to the point." She was no longer feigning a smile. "You're treading out of your league here. You have no idea what you're playing with."

"I beg to differ."

"I see." She looked around. "If you're here then that must mean you know about him."

I straightened up. "Yes."

"You may be happy with him now, but one day when you're not looking, he'll hurt you, and he'll hurt you deeply." She sounded impatient. "Part of him is a monster."

I wanted to shut her up. I felt that surge again. She cleared her throat again and again and coughed slightly. Then she coughed louder. I realised I had balled my hands into a fist and immediately opened them. She cleared her throat one last time, a puzzled look on her face.

I lifted my shoulders and faced her.

"You may see him as a monster, but he is not. He's a beautiful, wonderful person."

Her steel blue eyes dimmed a little.

"You're right. I see my son for what he actually is. He did try to kill me, and because of that, I pushed him away, but I see too a great man with a lot of potential in the business world. You look like a smart girl." She walked closer. "My son has a certain path chosen for him, and it unquestionably does not collide with yours. As C.E.O. of Jaeger Group, he has to forge bonds with a lot of people if he's to move to greater heights. That bond includes getting married to someone of equal calibre who can take him there. Aiden is spoken for, and like a smart girl, you should know what that means."

My evening had been instantly ruined by two words.

"Make sure to let Aiden know I was here and tell him Charlotte sends her love."

She turned around gracefully and walked away.

Aiden was spoken for. It was the punch line to the whole joke. I knew it had been too perfect to be true. What had I been thinking?

I thought it would be unwise for me to just give a conclusion without hearing from Aiden, so I decided to wait for him instead of running away like my heart begged me to. I headed for the library, unable to think clearly. It was dimly lit, just like the first time I saw it. Nothing had changed except there were no books on the table. My eyes wandered to the white door. Behind it was a holding cell for Aiden. I tiptoed toward it and stopped some steps away. I wanted to go in but refrained myself. What would I gain by seeing such a place?

I backed away and moved from shelf to shelf, checking out the collections of books. I selected a book from the 'African mythology' section and started reading.

"I figured I would find you here."

I didn't know time had flown by so fast. Aiden adjusted his tie.

"I never knew stories like these existed. There are so many myths and legends here, enough to wrinkle my brain."

"We learn as we go."

We stared at each other without saying anything.

"Your mother was here."

"I know."

His right hand settled in one pocket.

"And even if Henry hadn't told me I would know. The smell of Chanel still hangs in the air."

"She is stunning."

"Yes, she is."

His eyes narrowed.

"You're sad."

His conclusion made me jittery. I was trying so hard to come off as composed.

"What did she do?"

"She said a few things which I agree with. You're spoken for and ..."

"Spoken for?" He grimaced.

"Yes."

"If I was, then I should have known."

"Your mother... Well, it doesn't matter. I have thought about it, and we shouldn't be together any longer than we need to be."

"What?" He clenched his jaw.

"I think it is best..."

"Don't you dare say that," he snapped. I thought he was going to hit the desk, but he circumnavigated it to reach me and sat on the table, leaving me no room to move away.

"Do you actually think I would let my mother dictate my life?"

Ignoring his obviously rhetorical question I said almost undaunted by his reaction, "I'm going to send in my resignation and move to Ghana. My godfather runs a private hospital there. He'll be more than happy to have me."

Aiden's features softened. "Don't leave me, please."

My heart skipped a beat.

"I have to."

"Why? Because of something that is clearly a lie?"

"No, it's not that alone. They are going to come for me whoever they are. And when they do they'll come for you too. Femi said they needed us both. Don't you get it?"

"No, I don't. But I can defend myself." He tried to assure me.

"How can you protect yourself when you could not fight me off, and I know nothing about being a witch?"

"Because I love you."

He went on his knees and pulled the swivel chair closer, so I faced him directly. His hands rested on my thighs. I resisted the urge to rake my fingers through his hair and then kiss him silly if only to take away his sadness.

He continued talking. "I cannot let you go. Don't condemn me to another hell."

"That's not what I want."

"Then say you'll stay." His hands encircled me with ease. "No one in their right minds will ever let you go. I am yours and no one else's."

I was physically and emotionally paralysed. He took my face in his hands and kissed me for a brief moment.

"I'll protect you even if it costs me my life."

I collapsed against his body, and he held on real tight. But doing that failed to drive away all my doubts. Those mixed feelings were still there.

CHAPTER 14

Femi and I were having lunch on a bright Tuesday afternoon at his place, and he kept on talking about how he wanted to get a new car and give me his current one.

"I don't want your car. Don't be offended."

"I'm not. I just don't understand why you don't want one."

He reached for his glass of wine. He did not give up his quest, "the Nissan still runs great. If you change your mind, I'll be ready to give it to you."

"I forget, aren't you here temporarily?"

"I've changed my mind. I've transferred to the agency here in Orient city."

He cleaned his hands with a napkin.

"Still on the serial abduction case?" I asked, giving up on the food in front of me and focused on the orange juice.

"Yes."

"No news on the kidnappers?"

"Not yet, but I do have a connection."

"What connection?"

He lowered his voice to a whisper.

"Ever since that night you were attacked, no one else has gone missing."

"That's odd."

"I know. Although the other women have not been found, I'm ninety per cent sure their abductors were your attackers. It's just strange that the random kidnappings stopped."

"You mean they were seeking me out?"

"Yes."

My thoughts became frenzied as I digested what Femi told me. The innocent women who knew nothing and still were abducted could be dead and all of it just to get to me.

"Have you told anyone about this?"

"No."

He straightened up and looked out the window.

"Why not?"

"You want me to tell my boss that an occult group needs you to revive a two-century-old witch who's gonna go on a killing spree once she's released? He may be superstitious but not that superstitious."

I relaxed my aching shoulders.

"Then what are you going to do?"

"See to your safety."

"Well, you're doing a good job."

He turned on the television, and the eloquent beauty who hosted the afternoon show came on.

"Would it be appropriate to ask why you did not kill Aiden when you had the chance? I'm sure you must have had chances or the chance to create one."

He waited a while before answering.

"Because... Because I changed. When I started working with Zeppelin agency, I was entrusted with lives, to protect them. I could not bring myself to take a life, although I knew the pain I was going through was unbearable." His voice became unsteady. "And I can't kill him even though now I hate his guts. I've seen the way you look at him, he makes you happy, and I will not be the one responsible for taking away your happiness."

I hesitated before saying, "thank you."

"But why him? You loved me once."

"Perhaps, but he is the one. Every fibre of my being knows it."

"I don't understand."

"It's not meant to be understood. I know you'll find someone else who will make you feel the same way Aiden makes me feel," I told him placing both my hands on the table.

"And what if I told you I want no one else?" he asked, his broken smile almost erasing the sullen look shadowing his face.

"Femi..."

My phone started to ring.

"Mrs Eneje."

"Simi....."

Her voice made it clear she had been crying.

"What's wrong?"

"It's Jessica. She's in St. Louis."

"What's she doing in the hospital?"

She sniffed in before answering.

"There was an accident. It was my fault, my fault."

"Is she alright?"

"Yes. The doctor said she'll be fine."

"I'll be there in twenty minutes."

Femi, who had been keenly watching me, asked, "What's happened?"

"It's my niece. Can you take me to St. Louis?"

"Sure. Is she okay?"

"She will be."

Femi got me to the hospital in record time, and we were directed to the Dolphin ward for children. My sister sat on the wicker chair besides Lisa, and she looked ten times her age. Her eyes were reddened and swollen. She stood up and hugged me as I walked in with Femi. There was a nurse giving drugs to a young boy in the next cubicle, and she turned around to face us.

"It's alright," she told us. "She'll be fine. Don't worry."

I took a careful look at Lisa, who had an IV on her left arm and bandages on her legs. There were cuts and scrapes on her face and hands, and her hair had been completely shaved off. I was betrayed by the tears I was trying to hold back.

"Femi," Ava finally acknowledged his presence as if she had just seen him.

Femi replied, "Don't cry anymore. She'll be fine."

Ava gave a weak smile, which quickly disappeared just as it had come.

"What happened?"

Ava explained slowly but not without difficulty. She had been so busy at the spa she forgot to go pick up her daughters up from school, and Lisa had wanted to get lunch from a restaurant only to get run down by a car.

"The driver sped away and could not be identified." Ava clasped her hands together.

"I'll get to the bottom of this I promise you," Femi assured her.

"Thank you," I muttered with a shaky voice.

I took the next day off work, promising to make up for it in full and joined my sister at the hospital to keep watch over my niece. I must have slept off because I was stirred back to reality by warm hands around mine.

"I'm sorry I woke you up," Aiden apologised.

I sat up yawning.

"It's alright." I looked around but could not find Ava.

"Where's my sister?"

"She's downstairs getting something to eat. I had to force her down there. She's forgotten she has to take care of herself too."

"She worries a lot. Even over simple things."

I glanced at Lisa, who was sound asleep.

"Thanks."

"How's she?"

"She's fine. She woke up for a few seconds and called for Mona." A smile found its way to my lips.

"How did you know I was here?"

"Jephery."

"Oh."

He removed a hair strand hanging loose from my face.

"I'm glad you're here."

"You have to get something to eat."

"I will."

"I have to go. Got urgent business to attend to. Please eat," he added as an afterthought.

"That's fine by me."

Ava came back into the ward a short while after Aiden left and brought me a sandwich and a bottle of water.

"Thank you."

"Did you see Aiden?"

"Yes."

She dragged a plastic chair closer and slumped into it, fatigue written all over her.

"It appears you have two men competing over your heart."

"Is it that obvious?" I asked, removing the bottle top.

"Yes. Anyone can see that."

"Well, I just have to make a choice now don't I?"

"I don't think so. From my point of view, you've already made that choice."

No more valid words had ever been spoken to me.

I spent all day the next day covering up for the shifts I had forfeited. The amount of work left me so tired I slept at the hospital. My next rota was in the morning after which I went home, took a long needed bath and changed into some comfy clothes. On getting to the children's ward at St. Louis, I was met with an empty bed.

My heart stopped. What had happened? A wave of nausea hit me as I pictured the worse. I took two steps at a time back to the admissions office only to be waylaid by Aiden.

"I can't find my sister or my niece."

"Don't worry love, they're still here."

"What do you mean?"

"I had your niece moved to a private room."

I felt relieved, only to become worried again.

"Why a private room? What happened?"

"I was here yesterday. Your sister was complaining about the noise from the other patients, so I made a call."

I had nothing to say. It was either I thanked him for making my niece more comfortable or scold him for using his influence to get what he wanted.

"Your sister is happy, which I know in turn will definitely make you happy." I gave up my quest to protest.

He led me to a different section of the hospital, where the crowd was considerably less. The room was painted blue with a variety of animals on every corner, and the window was closed to keep in all the cold air. An assortment of flowers neatly arranged nearly covered half the room. Lisa was awake and by her side was Mona playing with her bald head. My sister and her husband occupied the sofa next to the bed.

We exchanged greetings, and I went over to Jessica's side and kissed her forehead.

"You gave us quite a scare, missy," I told her.

"Sorry." She apologised, smiling sheepishly. "Thank you, Mr Aiden, for the flowers. They are beautiful."

I watched as Jephery and my sister thanked Aiden and watched them laugh over a silly joke Mona made.

It gave me a warm feeling right in my gut and heart. My phone rang. It was Doctor Osayande. His shaky voice conveyed a rather short and brusque message. He wanted me in his office immediately. I had to leave for St. Cloud even though I wanted to stay.

"I'm needed at the hospital."

Aiden looked up at me with laughing eyes.

"I'll take you there," he said, standing up. Ava and Jephery exchanged a look. She winked at me and smiled awkwardly.

"Can't you stay a little longer?" Lisa asked Aiden. "You can stay until it's time for visitors to leave."

Aiden looked my way.

"Far be it from me to make a beautiful girl sad. I'll stay," he told a happy Jessica.

"And I'll take a cab. I'll call you when I get off work."

I said my goodbyes to everyone and rushed out. It took me a while to get a cab, and when I arrived at St. Cloud, I was praying not to get a scolding from the Medical Director. His bloodshot eyes when he was angry made even the strongest of hearts uncomfortable.

"Hold it!" I screamed at Doctor Warren, who just entered the elevator. He quickly barred the closing doors. "Thank you," I said, hand on my heaving chest.

"Nurse Oladeji, why are you in such a hurry?"

"I've been summoned by the boss. That was thirty minutes ago."

I punched in the floor number and breathed slowly.

I got off the elevator when it reached the fourth floor, and half ran to the end of the west corridor. I knocked on the door that had the Director's name boldly written in a nondescript font.

"Come in," a voice ordered.

I opened the door, and every breath in me got sucked from my lungs. I knew who they were immediately. There was one in the chair meant for the Medical director and three others, but I only recognised the one they had called Bode. Doctor Osayande was standing there beside him, looking like a scared ram about to be slaughtered for Sallah.

"Welcome Nurse, we've been expecting you," the man in the chair said, smiling a wicked smile. I swallowed hard and felt the hair on my hands stand up.

"Come on in."

I had a mind to run out, but he guessed what I was about to do and slammed the table with his fist. "You had better come in and close the door."

"Simi, I'm sorry, but they threatened my family if I didn't get you here."

"Keep quiet." The man spoke quietly to Doctor Osayande. "I'm Kolade. Now that we've gotten that out of the way I'll get straight to the point. We're going to leave this hospital together and if anyone questions you on the way, tell them I'm your relative or come up with a better excuse."

"We'll never leave without alerting suspicion," I said, taking a careful perusal of the faces of the men.

"Oh, you mean your bodyguards? They are but little fishes, and we fried them without wasting time. But they're still alive if you're worried, just not very conscious."

I reached for the door. Bode was at my side in quick motions. He grabbed my hand, and I grabbed his back, a burning rage filling my stomach. My body and mind were no longer mine. Bode's arm caught on fire. He ran from me, hitting it against the wall. The two other men fell on the ground coughing up blood while the medical director cowered on the floor and called on God to save him.

With a wave of my hand, I picked up a surprised Kolade from his chair and pulled him toward me. He held on to his neck, struggling to get free. He stopped fighting despite the pain he was in and let go of his neck. He dug out a beaded string from his pocket which he threw around my wrist. It burnt me badly, and my grip on Kolade loosened. I could feel the power within me restrained.

The men stopped coughing, and Kolade regained his stance. I tried to run out again, but Kolade held my hair and pulled me back. He laughed joyously. "You really are the one. But you try that again or try to escape," Kolade cautioned, "we'll start breaking every bone in your body just like your Meje beast of a saviour did to my arm."

My eyes flew up in surprise. I should have known they would find out about Aiden.

"What..."

"Bode stand up!"

Bode managed to put out the fire and stood up.

Kolade ordered them to wait for us in the car.

"Be a good girl and behave," he whispered as we walked out of the room.

We were almost through the waiting room and out the front door when Nadia yelled my name.

"Oladeji, where are you off to? "

"I'm helping Mr Kolade to his car."

"I should have known, always helping people when it's not even required of you."

The man threw Nadia a smile. I tried to communicate with Nadia with my eyes, but she did not see it. Kolade gave me a nudge, and I smiled along.

"I'll be back soon."

"What was that all about?" Kolade asked in a ruthless tone as soon as Nadia was out of earshot.

"Just two friends talking. I wasn't trying anything."

I was thrown into the back a jaguar and forced to drink a white substance. The entire car began spinning, and I felt sick in my stomach. I was losing consciousness fast.

"Aiden," I cried out in a faint voice. And then total darkness.

CHAPTER 15

Something fast paced was happening around me, but I could not tell what. My hands were held tight in an awkward position, and it hurt. A few minutes later, the fog cleared from my eyes and I could see everything. It was an area surrounded by tall trees and lit up with large red candles. The ground was littered with fallen leaves, and the air smelled of compost and something sweet. I was closer to the bank of a large body of water. There were six other people tied up on the ground far from me, only one of them was a man.

Of the people on their feet, there were more men than women. I counted them. They were twenty and all dressed in white overalls with amulets around their necks. One of the women inspected the bodies on the ground and then joined the other men. My arms were becoming number by the second.

I wriggled around using my fading strength. The ropes did not budge or show any sign of loosening up. I cursed my captors under my breath and coughed.

The last light of the sun disappeared and night settled upon the earth like a boding sign.

"Who's there? What is happening there? This is the Oni National Park. No one should be here at this time."

Oni National Park was located at the outskirts of Ibadan. They had taken me to where I assumed it had all started.

The light from the torch shone through the trees and rested on me. I squinted away from it and coughed some more. The owner of the voice came through the final row of trees. He put off his torchlight and observed the area.

"Our father in heaven." He made the sign of the cross and brought out a walkie-talkie from his pocket. "Security..." was the last thing he said before someone came behind him and knocked him out.

"An additional sacrifice is not a bad thing." The man who hit him laughed wickedly.

I found my voice at last. "Just let him go, he didn't do anything!" "She's awake," someone said.

"Just let him go," I repeated.

"I'm afraid we can't do that," Kolade said coming out of the crowd. "It's time," he announced.

"Time for what?"

The full moon rose above the trees, and its reflection fell on the water. Kolade made everyone take their places next to it. He stood at the head of the semi-circle and brought out a calabash adorned with cowries. He spoke into it and made his way towards me with a knife.

"What are you doing?"

"The first rites have already been carried out. This is a vital part of the final ritual," he explained. I remembered something.

"Well, I know you can't perform your ritual without another key ingredient."

I was trying to buy some time, but for what reason, I had no idea. I figured sooner or later I would be found; perhaps more dead than alive.

"What do you mean?" he asked curiously.

"I know my blood is not the only thing you need here. You need someone else's."

"What else do you know?" My method of stalling was working.

"I know there's only one surviving person with the Meje blood flowing through his veins and I know you need him."

"You have gained some knowledge, but you're wrong. We don't need him, well we didn't anymore because our powers have grown immensely and you are practically the essence of Ajë, and it is more than enough. You see, we have been monitoring you ever since our unfortunate run-in with the beast. I am so sure he'll be coming here to your rescue."

"Please leave him out of this," I cried, now more afraid for Aiden's safety than for mine. Kolade only laughed. I had never felt so much hate for a person.

"I'm sorry, but we can't leave him out of this. We left him some clues for him to get here and I'm sure he will. Ajë will need to have her revenge on the people who put her away. Like you said, he is a key ingredient, for her first meal in years."

"Why are you doing this?"

"Power, my sweet girl, power. But right now it's no concern of yours. It's time," he said curtly and proceeded to make a significant cut on my hand. I muffled a shriek and breathed rapidly. He placed the calabash under my bleeding hand to let the blood flow in. Then he proceeded to make several cuts on my legs and my face.

"Please stop," I pleaded.

Kolade went on without giving me a second glance. He was back at the head of the circle, calabash in hand. The gathering all took turns cutting their hands and putting drops of their blood into the calabash. Kolade was the last, after which he took it and placed it in on the ground. They all knelt down facing the lake and Kolade began an incantation where for every juncture he would place his hands inside the calabash and then wash his blood off with the water from the lake.

Íbi jiga ti Orun!
Ipetele ibi ti Aye!
Ma lo jeje ki o le da bi Iji!
Dawo duro ki o dabi omi to o son worowo!
Ajë! Olobukun eyan ti o mu ore ofe to mu Imole wa!
Bawa rin ni onon ti o mo, ti o si Okukun ni be!

I watched all this unfold with my heart in my mouth. 'I was going to die' was the only thought in my head. I looked from my left to my right when I noticed a sudden chill in the air.

The surface of the lake gave a bubbling sound and stopped. Kolade placed both his feet into the shallow part of the water and continued with his incantations. The bubbling resumed in full force as if the water was boiling. A white cocoon-like substance came bursting through the surface. The cocoon-like material touched the ground, and the gathering sauntered towards it. A white staff fell out of it before the frail woman who looked too familiar. She was caught by Kolade.

"Ajë."

He looked at her like she was a newborn baby.

Her hair was whiter than her garb, her lips a dark blue and her skin appeared to be covered in scales. Kolade spoke to her in Yoruba, but it did not sound like the one I understood. She looked at the tied up abductees on the floor and was aided by Kolade toward them. She took a careful glance at the first man and what happened next frightened me so much my teeth began to clatter.

The witch bent down and sunk her protruding fangs into the hand of the man. There was no struggle from him. Her scales were becoming less prominent. She took her time with all seven of them, her mouth soaked with so much blood. Her followers were on their knees again and watched on in awe. Her fangs retracted when she was done.

"How can you kneel there and just watch?" I screamed, my fear now replaced by anger.

The witch turned her glare towards me. Kolade whispered something to her, and she smiled. She drifted in my direction with poise and grace, her staff by her side.

"Daughter of Ireti Eniola, we meet face to face," she said, moving her eyes from my head and down to my toes. I wondered how she was able to speak English so fluently, but I had seen stranger things in the last few months that made it trivial in comparison.

"Untie her," she ordered one of the men who hurriedly did in an attempt to impress. He bowed and backed away. I flexed my arm.

"Get up," she said to me.

I hesitated. Without warning, a crushing pain erupted in my chest. My screams could be heard miles away. I wondered why in God's name, I was alive to feel something so horrifying.

"Daughter of Ireti, don't fight it."

It felt like my heart was being held by a firm unrelenting grip, and that hand was gradually pulling it away from my body.

"I'm simply taking what's mine," the witch said in a soothing voice. She came down to my prone position and held my head up. The pain was so much I could not cry; I could only wish for death to come quickly. She stared directly into my bulging eyes and then the pain was gone.

I fell to the floor and was left there. Tears came flowing freely as I thought about all the things I had not done with my life. Yet among all, one seemed to take priority. I knew I would regret it if I died without telling Aiden I loved him. If only I were not dying. I could still see the witch walking away in a foggy haze and then the image was gone.

***

When I opened my eyes, all I could see and feel was weighty darkness. In a few seconds, my vision became more transparent, and I could make out what was behind and ahead of me. I was in a small canoe. The canoe moved on its own accord going with the flow of the water. It soon came to a stop. The ground was full of broken works of clay, and even though I stepped on it with my bare feet, it did not hurt. There was a straight path whose end I could not see. It was enclosed on both sides by large winding plants with black leaves. Everything appeared surreal, even the sky which seemed to be absent and was replaced by a thick cloud of smoke. I walked down the path for a long time, expecting each time I heard a whooshing sound a demon or monster.

At the end of the path were more broken pieces of earthenware, and in the middle of it was a tree. Its top could not be seen because it disappeared into the cloud of smoke. Its thick broad roots rose in and out of the ground in a zigzag pattern.

A small figure ran around the base of the tree. I edged closer with caution. The apparition moved away, and I could no longer see it. The sound of laughter echoed in the damp air. It sounded like a child laughing. I climbed over a root toward the pealing laughter. It stopped, and I halted on my tracks. The laughter started again only this time it was behind me. I took a sharp turnaround to find a boy no more than five years old behind me. A black and red cloth covered his small body. His brown eyes and his chubby cheek made him look harmless.

"Hey," I gasped. "What are you doing here? Are you alright?"

He tilted his head.

"What is this place?" He did not answer. I looked around. Nothing made sense.

"Do you know where we are?" I asked. "Do you speak English?"

The boy looked up from his bare feet and smiled.

"Am I dead?"

He stretched out his hand.

"You want me to take your hand?"

He slowly nodded.

I took his hand, and he dragged me along with him, dodging the roots as we went around the enormous tree trunk.

"Slow down," I said.

For a child, he had the agility and strength of an older person. He stopped abruptly, and I did too. My eyes went in the direction of where his gaze lingered. There was a hole in the tree, enough to let me pass through if I bent over. The boy yanked at my hand again and dragged me along into the entrance. He let go of me once we were halfway inside.

I saw a light at the end of the tunnel and moved towards it. The tunnel opened up to a cavernous chamber. At the far end stood a large stone chair adorned with skulls. The place was illuminated by lights from the gaping mouths of more heads.

On the stone chair sat an old man smoking a pipe. The smoke coming out of his mouth formed only one pattern; a skull. The cloth on him was a lengthier version of the boy's, only he wore a wide-brimmed straw hat which shielded his eyes. I looked around for the boy, but he was nowhere to be found.

"Welcome, Iwir," the old man's voice boomed across the room.

"Where am I?" I asked.

"Where do you think you are?" He removed his pipe from his mouth.

"I don't know," I answered truthfully.

There was a pause, and then I asked again what had been bothering me ever since I found myself on the mysterious canoe.

"Am I dead?"

"A stranger has eyes but do not see."

I was beginning to get annoyed by his evasive answers.

"I think I'm dead," I stated for my own benefit.

"Hmmm..."

"Where is this place?"

He puffed on his pipe and spoke. "Orun-apadi, the unseen land of potsherds. It is the path taken before reaching the spirit world. But I doubt you are dead. I would know."

"So I'm not dead?"

"It is doubtful."

"Who are you?" I ventured to ask.

He did not answer immediately.

"I am known as the trickster."

"The god of duality," a quiet laughing voice said behind me.

I looked back to find the boy, and then he was gone in a flash.

"The guide of travellers, the god of beginnings."

The old man was back on his chair.

"The Orisha of death," the boy said in front of me faintly, but it was strong enough to make me come to grips with who I was dealing with.

"And so on and so forth. I am Eshu, Iwir," the old man revealed, taking a drag of smoke out of his pipe.

"I thought you were just a myth. You and all the other Orishas I have recently come to know."

"Time is a myth, but I am not. We are all but forgotten, but that does not mean we have stopped existing."

"And why am I here?"

"You're not supposed to be here," he explained.

"I don't understand."

"You're here because of him."

He looked past me. I slowly turned around and found to my greatest surprise, Aiden walking up the tunnel. His eyes widened when he saw me.

"What are you doing here?" he asked, rushing over to me and throwing his arms around me.

"If you're here too then that means you're probably dead," I said breaking away from his embrace.

"I'm not dead. My soul was pulled into this world by Femi through some bizarre ritual to get to the axe of Sango. I never thought it would work, but here I am. He told me there would be consequences and I guess you being here is just the beginning."

"Why did you come here?"

"To get what we need to kill the witch."

"I thought she could not be killed."

"There's only one way to kill her." He looked at Eshu who pretended to not notice us.

"How?"

Aiden moved away from me and toward the god. "I am here for the weapon."

"You mean this weapon?" Eshu asked as an axe materialised out of thin air and into his hands. It was a double-headed axe with a curved handle. The metallic head reflected the light of the flames. "I cannot give it to you."

"I have come prepared to do anything you ask," Aiden said aloud.

The old man stood up for the first time. He was taller than anyone I had ever seen and seemed to get taller as he walked toward us. He took a long drag on his pipe.

"If you can answer my simple question, I may consider lending it to you."

"Agreed."

"And if you fail," Eshu put up a finger, "if you give me the wrong answer, cursed one, I will take possession of your soul and hers."

Aiden turned to me. I shook my head.

"Anyone can see the love you have for her? What would you do to save her?"

Aiden pursed his lips and then relaxed.

"Anything," he answered. "I would do anything for her."

"So be it."

The boy emerged behind Aiden, and the old man disappeared.

"You have only one try, cursed one. Dried smoked fish is delicious, but what is one to eat before the fish is smoked?"

The boy who I now believed to be Eshu waited for a reply patiently. I pondered over the question and came up with nothing.

"Aiden," I called.

"Don't worry, Simi, I'll figure it out," he told me and mouthed the question over and over again.

"Just one try?" Aiden asked.

"One try cursed one."

Aiden was in deep thought again, and for a long time, he mauled the question over in his mind, and so did I. I could only come up with one thing.

"Aiden, maybe it's a trick question. Maybe there is no definite answer."

That seemed to have done the trick because he said with all confidence, "I have your answer."

I froze.

"There is no answer to your question. Instead, it is a lesson. Dried smoked fish I believe represents the future and the fish not yet smoked represents the present. It means that while a person must think about his future, he must also remember to take care of the present."

The old man reappeared next to his chair.

"Well done, cursed one, you have answered my question."

I breathed a sigh of relief.

"The axe," Aiden demanded.

"I remember telling you if you answer my question, I may consider lending it to you. I did not come by this," he indicated the axe by a tilt of his head, "by accident. I came by it through careful planning and pure wit. It's not very safe for someone who tries to double cross the god of thunder. But I did, and I got away with it. Until recently. This weapon can kill anything and anyone, including the gods themselves. Including me."

He stopped and observed us.

"War is coming mortals, and you may all be caught in the crossfire. With this weapon which I have carefully protected for hundreds of years and a worthy army, I can be assured of victory. Now, why do you think I should give you my most prized possession?" His question was thrown at Aiden.

"Because I'm ready to give you my soul in exchange for the axe."

"Aiden, don't."

"I could easily take it."

"Not without a fight."

The god seemed amused. "I like you, cursed one, and because of this, I will heed your request. However, you have a time limit. I don't want anyone knowing the weapon is on earth," Eshu said and threw the axe at Aiden who caught it. "You both can leave."

The moment he said that I felt myself being pulled away by a tremendous force.

"Aiden!" I shouted, but he was already gone. I woke up with a gasp as if I had been drowning and had just come above water and received a blast of much-needed air. My throat was on fire, and my vision blurry. I was still on the ground. I leaned up to get a good view of the witch who now watched as the bodies of the dead men and the woman were thrown into a freshly dug hole.

There was a loud banging noise and from the dark emerged Femi and Aiden hand in hand. I could see the axe on Aiden's hand.

"Kill them!" Kolade yelled at his comrades. They were no match for Aiden or Femi who had come with a gun. He fired several shots which sent the birds flying out of their nests and me cowering in a corner. The noise died down, and I looked up. They were all down on the ground; dead or maimed, save for the witch and Kolade.

"A necessary sacrifice!" Kolade roared and stepped in front of the witch. That was the last thing he said before Aiden ripped off his head from his body and pushed him away. Aiden still looked the same, save for his silver locks.

The witch laughed loudly, and Aiden gave her no time for anything else. He lunged at her, but she was ready, and with one wave of her staff, she pushed Aiden away from her. The axe fell out of his hand when he hit the ground and into the midst of the bodies.

"Aiden!" I shouted half running, half crawling toward him.

"Stay back!" he shouted at me.

Femi, seeing a window of opportunity reloaded his gun and shot at her, but none had any effect on her. She sent Femi soaring through the trees. The loud thump made by his falling body would forever be etched into my memory. It sounded so ghastly I feared he might be dead.

Aiden made a move to reach for the axe, but the witch came up behind him and dragged him toward the lake by the hem of his shirt.

"Meje beast," she spat.

Aiden was defenceless against her. "I will reveal what you truly are."

She pushed him away from her. I needed to get to the axe but saw no way to reach it without being killed.

All my plans ceased when I heard Aiden screaming. My body went numb. I needed to help him. He was on his knees, holding his head. His hair grew longer as his clothes ripped from his body. Soon his entire body was covered in fur, and then the transformation was complete. His shouting had died down to growling. I watched the creature before me without blinking. Standing where Aiden had been a moment ago was a four-foot creature with yellow eyes, a black fur and a long silver mane. The witch who had been laughing during Aiden's transformation came closer to him and stroked his hair.

"You will do my bidding until I see it fit to kill you."

I found the strength to take a foot forward towards the axe.

"Kill her," she commanded.

I remained transfixed as the creature leapt in my direction and circled me as it would a prey. It charged at me and stopped as I fell to the ground, completely paralysed by fear.

"Aiden," I called as I came eye to eye with the creature. It made a snarling noise in response as it took some steps forward and a few backwards. It seemed to struggle with the task it had been assigned to it.

"Kill her!" The witch screamed again.

"Aiden, it's me," I spoke to the creature. "Do not do what she says."

The creature's eyes dimmed. It turned its attention toward the witch who was now fuming.

"I should know better than to expect results from Meje filth."

The creature dashed in the witch's direction. She waved her staff at him, but it had no effect. Stunned by this fact but unshaken, she stood her ground as the creature went for her throat. The witch's incantation became louder, which made the beast wriggle around on the ground wailing loudly.

"Die!" she shouted.

I was not going to let that happen.

There was a chance, and I took it. I picked up the axe, and with all the strength I could muster swung it at her back. There was an impact, but it came at a heavy cost. Her staff had gone through my stomach and out the back. She screeched like a banshee as she melted. Her wand disappeared into thin air.

I smiled as I coughed up blood.

Aiden's hands were there to catch me as I fell. I looked down on the gaping hole in my stomach, and then I saw his beautiful face as he placed his bleeding hand over my mouth.

"Drink up. I won't have you dying on me. Not now." I placed my bloodied hands on his face.

"Simi, I think I have to go now," he said. Part of him was already fading away.

"Aiden," I blurted out with effort. I wanted to tell him to stay, that it was going to be alright and we could finally be together.

"I love you," he said before completely disappearing. I had no strength to scream or move. I remained on the wet ground staring up into the starry night as I sobbed uncontrollably. It was the only thing I could do.

199

CHAPTER 16

A week passed, and I was still in my pyjamas. Nothing had changed. Aiden was gone, and I did not know what else to do. Nadia had come over and said something about how the word asshole was not written on the face of any man. My sister had chimed in too with stories of good men and said Aiden may not be the one after all. Femi had made up an excuse for my depression since I gave no explanation as to why I shut myself to the outside world; Aiden had broken up with me and left the country.

It was a depressing thought because no one would ever know how he saved my life, losing his in the process.

"You have to eat something," Femi said, and I sensed more tears coming. There was no way to stop it. "You don't have to kill yourself because he's gone."

He turned my face toward him and was met with a vacant stare.

"Why, Simi? He's gone! What other proof do you need?"

"He's not gone," I whimpered.

"Look," he said, lifting his shirt to reveal his upper body. There was no scar. No one would have known one was there a week ago and such a conspicuous one at that.

"But..." I tried to speak.

"But nothing Simi."

"You wanted this. You wanted him gone!"

"I admit I did, but I did not want him to die. I can't bear to see you do this to yourself."

"You planned it all."

"You have to accept he's gone for good."

"I hate you."

He looked shocked, but that look quickly faded away.

"I don't care. You have to live your life."

"Leave. Get out," I told him without raising my voice.

He hesitated before getting up from the only chair in my bedroom.

"I'll be back to check up on you." He sighed and walked out, dragging his feet behind him.

I wanted to be alone for as long as I could. Any contact with the outside world would only remind me of my pain. That night I dreamt of Aiden. He was smiling at me from a distance. When I awoke, I remembered his face as clear as day. For a moment, I thought he was still alive. It was the first time he had appeared in my dreams ever since he was taken away from me so cruelly.

I took a long bath scrubbing myself thoroughly and all the time wondering where I got the strength. I put on some clean clothes and headed out to Aiden's mansion. I was let in by Henry, who gave me a polite greeting.

"Are you alright?" he asked.

"I'm fine."

"Miss Simi," he started, "Master Aiden left me a series of instructions about a week ago. He told me if anything happened to him, I should carry out those instructions. He has not been back since then, and I'm beginning to doubt he'll ever come back."

I bit my lower lip to hold back the influx of tears. It was difficult not to cry.

"Should I go ahead carrying out his instructions?" He waited for a reply. "Yes, you can," I replied. "I'm just going to hang around for a while if you don't mind."

"I don't," he said and briskly walked away.

I lingered at the base of the staircase and became alarmed when I heard something shatter. There was silence and then more shattering. "Henry," I muttered in pity.

I slowly made my way up the stairs and found myself in Aiden's room. It smelled like him. I sat on the edge of the bed and gathered the blankets into my arms and inhaled deeply. Every ounce of my defeated being screamed for the pain I felt to go away, but it did not. I had brought myself here to be tortured by memories. I stared at nothing in particular and swallowed.

"Why did you have to do that?" I asked, staring at the painting on the wall. "You should not have given your life for mine. Now you're gone, and I'm confused. I don't know what to do with my life." I laughed bitterly. "I miss you so much. With every waking second, I miss you. What I would give to have you kiss me just one more time." I sobbed. "I'm slowly falling to pieces, and the pain doesn't seem to end. Why won't it end?"

When no answer was forthcoming, I answered myself. "Maybe it's because I keep expecting you to show up to rescue me. And right now I need some rescuing. This empty feeling is not going anywhere soon. My heart cannot go on like this. Nothing makes sense without you, so... so...please help me. I have no idea what to do. The day I lost you, I lost myself. I'm so lost."

There was another shattering sound.

"And the saddest part is that you left without knowing, without hearing me say those words you wanted to hear me say. I was trapped in something I could not understand, but I see clearly now. I love you more than I could possibly have imagined."

"Well, I've heard it now."

I stood up hastily with a hand on my rapidly beating heart. Maybe I had gone insane and finally conjured Aiden out of my head due to my loneliness. Because there he was, leaning against the door.

"Are you really here?"

"Yes."

Something was different about him, but I could not quite place it.

"Is this a dream?"

"No." He drew nearer.

"But you disappeared. I saw you disappear. How is this possible? You were gone."

He smiled.

I stretched out my hand, and he drew closer. I half expected my hands to pass through him, but he held on to them. He pulled me and put his arms around me. A surge of current ran through me when I felt his arms. He was real. More tears came pouring down, and more sobbing followed.

"Shhhh..." he consoled me.

"What happened?" I asked in between sobs.

"Eshu was not after my soul per se, he was after the creature's or whatever made me what I was. Since I harboured the creature, it had to be taken from me. He said it was a useful addition to his special army."

"Then why aren't you dead?"

"I am puzzled by it too. Although he told me he could not be a wastrel who uses a dog to stalk fish."

I chuckled in between my tears. It was all too good to be true. I held on tighter, not wanting to let go.

"So, it's over?" I asked.

"More or less. I'm here now."

I looked up at him. "I thought I would never see you again."

"I thought so, too, but here we are."

He leaned in closer and kissed me deeply. That erased every last doubt I had. It was really Aiden because no one else could mess with my head with such a simple action.

"Don't ever leave again."

"I promise."

I buried my head in his chest and continued to sob. He let me until I was satisfied. I felt lighter as if a heavy load had been lifted off me, and I was once again complete.

ABOUT ERHU

Erhu Kome Yellow is an Urhobo author of fantastical stories where gods, mythological creatures and magic come together.
She has been shortlisted for the Syncity Anthology prize, the Quramo Writers' Prize and featured in Blaud Magazine. Dawsk is her first book, and is currently the Creative Freelance Writers Book of the year.

CONNECT WITH ERHU

FB: https://www.facebook.com/Erhukomeyellow/
Tw: https://twitter.com/erhuwrites
IG: https://www.instagram.com/erhukome

OTHER BOOKS BY LOVE AFRICA PRESS

Queer and Sexy Collection Volume 1 by Eniitan

Ere's Secret and 223 Bonny Street by Firi Kamson

His Captive Princess by Kiru Taye

Love at First Sound by Amaka Azie

Unravelling His Mark by Zee Monodee

CONNECT WITH US

Facebook.com/LoveAfricaPress

Twitter.com/LoveAfricaPress

Instagram.com/LoveAfricaPress

www.loveafricapress.com